HEAR ME

A Fly By Boys Novel

H L MULLER

H. L. Muller is Australian, and this book is written in United Kingdom/Australian English.

ISBN: 978-0-6488610-4-1

Cover design by: Avdal Designs

Editing: Salt & Sage Books

Lyrics: Lukasz Muller

Sensitivity Read: Tia Edwards

Publisher: H. L. Muller

❀ Created with Vellum

For my readers, I wouldn't be here without you.

Playlist

These are some songs that Alintia and Joel listen too, and that
I enjoyed while writing this book.
I Want Crazy – Hunter Hayes
Love Story (Taylor's Version) – Taylor Swift
Move Along – The All-American Rejects
Everywhere – Michelle Branch
Why Won't You Love Me – 5 Seconds of Summer
Who's That Girl – Guy Sebastian, Eve
Rock Me – One Direction
Today Was A Fairytale (Taylor's Version) – Taylor Swift
Song On Fire – Nickleback
Play That Song – Train
Take My Breath Away – Berlin
Fallin' For You – Colbie Caillat
If I Had You – Adam Lambert
She Drives Me Crazy – Fine Young Cannibals
Senorita – Shawn Mendes, Camila Cabello
Latch – Disclosure, Sam Smith
Just the Girl – The Click Five
My Life Would Suck Without You – Kelly Clarkson

Prologue - Alintia

Why did I agree to this? Blind dates are hell on earth.

If it weren't for Chloe, my best friend since seventh grade, I wouldn't be here. Chloe is persistent that I find a decent man to date. In hindsight, the dates and boyfriends I have had were all wrong decisions and show that I have appalling taste in men. They were all total assholes—only interested in appearances and sex. That's not to mention the men that were racist pricks and wouldn't date me because I am Aboriginal. Honestly, I know I am better off without those men in my life, but it still hurts to know there are still people out there in Australia who believe that Aboriginal's are the pariahs here.

For a while now, Chloe has insisted I needed to meet this man she works with.

"He is the perfect man for you!" she had said to me. *"He is emotionally available for starters—unlike the other guys you have dated—and he is funny, quirky, and totally easy to talk to."*

If Chloe weren't a lesbian, I would think that she was in love with him herself with how much she gushed over him. But if he's so great, why wasn't he on time? I managed to arrive at Starbucks, order my coffee, and take up my seat against the wall with five minutes to spare. The cushioned seat's position allowed me to survey the entire shop for this "perfect man" without craning my neck.

In the spirit of blind dates, Chloe refused to show me his photo or tell me his name. The only markers I have to identify him are his brown hair and that he will be wearing a hat and pair of coloured Converse shoes. Wanting to dress up for this date, I have on a sunflower sundress that falls to my knees, black wedges, and my blonde and brown curls fall over my shoulder.

I check the time on my iPhone again—he is now eight minutes late. Several thoughts flick through my head at once. Did he see me and decide I wasn't worth meeting? Did he stand me up? Car crash? Traffic? Did he go to the wrong place?

Picking up my phone, I text Chloe.

Me: Your "amazing" co-worker is late! If he isn't here in ten minutes, I'm leaving.

Chloe: Stop stressing, not everyone is as punctual as you are—tight ass!

Sighing, I put my phone back on the table and pick up my Grande white mocha. As the sweet taste rolls over my tongue, I close my eyes and resist the urge to hum. Starbucks coffee is life. Am I falling into stereotypes? Yes. Do I care? No.

I glance around the shop—again—the positive attitude I had this morning quickly drying up as the time ticks by. I scroll through my phone, checking out Instagram, when someone sits down at the table next to mine. Ignoring them, I keep my attention on my phone—is it too cliché for me to take a photo of my coffee cup?

For a minute, they shift about, their wooden chair legs scraping against the ground.

"This was such a stupid idea," a gruff voice mutters.

Annoyance flashes through me at all their noise, and I look up. A white man with sun-kissed skin is sitting diagonally across from me with his back to the store. Shaggy brown hair is stuffed underneath a cap, a muscle singlet showing off long toned arms. His left arm is covered in tattoos. Shifting in my seat ever so slightly, I see black distressed skinny jeans and bright turquoise Converse.

It's him.

Chloe really wasn't lying when she gushed about how attractive he is.

"Finally!" I proclaim. "How long were you going to keep me waiting?"

"I'm sorry?" he questions, his deep voice rolling over me. His hazel eyes widen as he meets my gaze under his hat, shoulders hunched as he leans against his table. His clean-shaven jaw tenses, a small muscle popping out at the edge of his sharp jawline.

"We did say we would meet at eleven, right?" I smile softy. I don't want to come off too intense.

"We did?" He looks confused.

"Anyway, you are here now," I brush it off. Complaining about his tardiness won't do me any favours. "I'm Alintia, but you can call me Ali—almost everyone does."

"Friends call me Jay," he offers with an awkward hand gesture that I think is meant to be a wave.

Silently, Jay picks up his coffee and moves to sit at my table, his legs knocking into mine.

"Ali, it's nice to meet you," Jay says, a small smirk edging at the corner of his mouth.

"Thanks, I'm sorry if Chloe forced you into coming today. I'm really not as pathetic as however she made me sound."

Jay chuckles, humour sparkling in his eyes.

I'd never put any stock into insta-love, but insta-lust? Oh, yes.

I can just imagine him pinning me against a wall, claiming me, owning me. *Where did that thought come from?*

"Why don't we start fresh? I'll forget everything and you can tell me about yourself?" Jay asks.

"Ok, sure." I glance around the room, trying to think about something to say. "Uh. I'm twenty years old, I live in the Gold Coast, and I'm a singer."

"Really?" His eyes flicker with an emotion I cannot place.

"Yeah, nothing crazy good or anything. My mum is worried about me trying to make a living from it."

"She doesn't support you?" he asks, something akin to pity on his handsome face.

"No, she is great—her and my dad came to all my shows and concerts while growing up—but she just thinks I should have a backup. It can be pretty hard to get your foot in the door in the industry. Sure, these days you can just record and drop an album on Spotify independently, but I don't have a band. It's just me," I say with a shrug. "I have been trying for a while. I stopped by a studio open day and did a performance with both acapella vocals and with the studio band and they recorded it for me. I recently dropped that demo with a few recording studios, and I am waiting to hear anything from them. Even being backup vocals on someone else's album would be amazing."

"That's very admirable. It's good to see you are pursuing your dreams. Not enough people do that anymore."

I blush at his praise and take a sip of my mocha to give myself a second to think about what to say next.

"Well, I already know what you do for work—since you work with Chloe. What's something else about you?" I ask.

"Hmm. I have four brothers. I am the second eldest and a twin."

"Oh, your poor parents," I joke.

"It was a crazy house to grow up in, that's for sure," Jay says with a chuckle. His mouth spreads in a huge grin, like there is a joke in there that I don't know.

"Tell me about your tattoos?" I blurt out, overwhelmed with curiosity, glancing at the elaborate drawings on his arm. I have never really been interested in someone with tattoos before— but I can instantly see the appeal.

"Well, my sleeve is combined of a few different things. It started off with one artist using a swirling line, now every-where I travel to, I find an artist to add to it. In whatever why they think will match the theme.

"It looks amazing."

"Do you have any tattoos?" Jay asks.

"No, I wish. My dad is pretty against them. So I grew up being told not to get any." I shrug. "I have never settled on a design I wanted enough to justify the argument of getting one, to be honest. Maybe one day when I fall in love with a tattoo then I will get one."

My phone buzzes across the table, interrupting our conversation, and I realise an hour has passed. The number isn't saved in my phone, and I am tempted to let it go to voice message, but something in my gut tells me I should answer now.

"I'm sorry," I apologise to Jay while swiping to answer the call and bring my phone to my ear.

"Hello?" I ask.

"Good afternoon, is this Alintia?" a feminine voice rings through the phone.

"Yes, how can I help you?"

"Alintia, my name is Rachel, and I am calling from Reckless Tunez. I would have called your agent, but you didn't have one listed on your submission."

"Really? This is really Reckless?"

She laughs gently. "Yes, we were hoping you could come in today with your agent to discuss your demo?"

"Oh, wow." I take a deep breath, turning away from the shop to cut out the noise. "Yes, I can. What time?"

"As soon as you can. Do you know our studio address?"

"Yes."

"Ok, great. We will see you soon!"

Rachel terminates the call and I lean back into my seat, releasing a big sigh.

"Is everything ok?" Jay asks, jolting me out of my thoughts. I had forgotten he was here. His face twists in pain, but I don't have time to think about that.

"Y-Yes. I think so. I—I need to go. I'm sorry."

I stand up, hastily collecting my handbag and empty coffee cup, leaving the table.

"Alintia?" Jay calls after me as I make my way out of Star- bucks, throwing my empty cup in the rubbish bin as I pass it, and out onto the street.

I don't turn around or look at him—I don't have time. I need to get halfway across the city. I'll get his number from Chloe later to apologise and explain. He will understand. This could be my big break!

One - Joel

EIGHT MONTHS LATER.

"J? Are you ready to go yet?" my twin brother, Charlie, calls from behind my closed bedroom door.

"Yeah, yeah, keep your pants on!" I grumble, shuffling over to the door while pulling my hat on.

Our band, Fly By, has a meeting with our manager today since our tour is starting up in a few months, and Charlie is always paranoid about being late. I may or may not be the chronically late twin. The only time I am not late is on tour, and that's only because I have a manager literally dragging me around sometimes. My four brothers and I made our band Fly By when we were teenagers and got famous a few years ago when we won the TV competition *'What It Takes!'*

Even with our fame, we have all kept pretty low-key and respect others and do our best to respect their time. I have to be on time, can't be drunk, can't be disrespectful. We were raised to be gentlemen, and we adapt that into our lives as famous rock stars. After we won *What It Takes!* we were on tour for two years—and don't get me wrong, it was amazing—but this last year we have had a well needed break. I have spent my time getting back in touch with nature, spending my days out in the bush hiking or camping out under the stars, and of course, writing new music. As much as I have loved exploring, I am looking forward to getting back out there with my brothers and performing for our fans—or the *Flyers*, as they started calling themselves.

I exit my bedroom and find Charlie sprawling on the couch, scrolling through his phone.

"Stalking Gwen's new boyfriend again, are you?" I tease him. Gwen has been his best friend—outside of me and our brothers—for fifteen years. And I think for about ten of those he has been in love with her.

"Psh, no," Charlie scoffs. He quickly locks his phone so I cannot see the screen and tucks it away in his pocket.

I worry for him sometimes. How long is too long to hold onto a dream that won't happen? Gwen has never given any of us any inclination that she returns his feelings, let alone even knows how he feels.

Even though his love makes him miserable, at least he can spend time with the girl he likes. There's this girl who has taken up residence in my head for eight months, despite the fact that I've only met her twice.

I met her by chance at a Starbucks in the city. I made the foolish decision to go out in broad daylight and was swarmed by fans and paparazzi. After a few quick turns in the shopping centre, I escaped for a whole second and used it to duck into the nearest shop. I bought a coffee and sat down with my back to the room to collect myself before I could make my way back to my car.

I can't even remember now why I needed to go out that day now, but I remember everything about *her*. She struck up a conversation with me, and I was sceptical that she was another fan who wanted something from me. However, as we got chatting, I realised she thought I was a date she was supposed to meet—or that's how it appeared at first. After the second time I met her, I wasn't so sure.

I didn't want to tell her that I wasn't this guy her friend had set her up with. I wanted to get to know her—to be this man she was supposed to meet. But then she bolted out of there, as if she didn't care to ever see me again. I wonder if she even remembered me.

"J, bro, you coming?" Charlie asks, pulling me out of my memories. He had gotten off the couch while I was lost in my mind and is holding the elevator doors for me.

We leave the apartment and head down to the garage in our private elevator to where our cars are. Since we are going to the same meeting, we pile into my baby—my black 2019 Subaru XV.

"Last point of business for this meeting," Mitch, our band manager, says. "Reckless Tunez has finalised negotiations for your opening act." He rolls out a promo poster, and I feel a lead ball drop to the pit of my stomach. I see her eyes first. A blue as bright as a summer sky, made even more enchanting by the contrast to her light brown skin. Dark brown hair with blonde ends—it should be unruly ringlets, but they have straightened it out to fall over her breasts. They have dressed her in a long flowing sundress, hinting at the curvy frame silhouetted by the dress. Standing at the front of the group, two men on her right and a woman behind her on her left. It's the country-pop band that Reckless Tunez created eight months ago.

"This is Afterglow," Mitch says, waving his hand at the poster. "Afterglow is a new up and rising band that are also managed by Reckless, and they will be joining you on tour." Mitch explains.

"What?" I ask, stunned.

"As they are funding the tour, the label gets the say, and Reckless want to promote Afterglow to your fanbase."

"But they are a completely different genre! How is that going to work with the *Flyers*?" I protest. "That's just not going to work!"

"How do you even know who they are?" my youngest brother, Ethan, asks. "I have never heard of them."

"That's irrelevant!" I state. *She* is the lead singer of Afterglow, my Alintia—not *my* Alintia. How am I meant to exist in her orbit without getting drawn in and hurt again?

"Joel, unless you have a valid reason why Afterglow shouldn't be the opening act, you're going to have to swallow your complaints and be a professional." Mitch gives me a stare that says, "I mean it," before turning back to the rest of my brothers. "We will finalise everything for the new album at our next meeting, but so far, recording is going well. And we think 'Runaway' will be one of the biggest hits on the album. We are going to drop it as a single first—probably in a month."

That song wasn't meant to see the light of day. I wrote it about Alintia after we first met, and Charlie overheard me playing around with the melody. One thing led to another and apparently now it will be the lead single on the new album. Don't get me wrong, I am happy to contribute to the album and band—I just wish it wasn't the song about her.

"Good," my oldest brother, Maverick, exhales. "Are we done?"

I tune out my brothers, my thoughts turning inwards, and—try as I had to resist—think about Ali. My mind goes back to the second time I met her, in this exact room, actually. About a month after I met her at Starbucks, I had to come in to record vocals for an older recording. As I was about to go into the booth with the sound techs, Mitch asked me to join him in a meeting. Networking and meeting new people are a big part in our lives, so it was nothing new for me. By this time, I had figured out that she had been signed to Reckless and—if I am being honest with myself—was hoping to run into her in the studio and pick up where that random date left off. I was thinking of how we could laugh over who she was meant to meet, and the stories of how we met that we could tell people. I walked into the room, and I can remember how my stomach filled with butterflies, seeing her in person again—this interesting and beautiful woman who I had such a great connection with—was overwhelming. Before I could say anything, she opened her mouth and broke my heart. In a few months, I will be face to face with her again and I don't know what to do with that information. How is it that someone I barely know can have my body twisted up into so many knots?

I half-register that Maverick leaves the meeting, leaving me with my three other brothers and Mitch.

My brothers and I formed our band, originally called the Watson Brothers, when I was thirteen, and often I look back and wonder how we were ever this lucky. It all started when

Maverick had to learn guitar for music lessons in high school, and we all realised how amazing making music is. Seven years, a change of our band name, a record deal, and an international tour later, we are one of the most famous bands in our time.

Maverick is the guitarist, I am lead vocals, Charlie is our drummer, our younger brother Tom is on bass, and the baby Ethan is on keyboard. I call him a baby, but he is almost eighteen. Mum had us all within the span of five years. Sometimes I wonder how my mum stayed sane, but we have a pretty amazing family unit, and I wouldn't change it for anything. And yes, if it wasn't obvious, our mum loves Tom Cruise. It's who we are all named after, and how we got the name for our band. I still think we should have called it "Great Balls of Fire," but that didn't go over well with my family.

Ethan clicks his fingers in front of my face, drawing me back to our meeting room.

"What?" I grunt.

"Are you ready to go, or do you want to stare into space all day?" he asks mockingly. Charlie and Tom glance at me as they gather their stuff.

"Yeah, I'm good." I stand and make my way out of the meeting room, saying goodbye to Mitch and the receptionist, Rachel, as I pass them.

The upcoming tour that I have been itching for now has a grey cloud hanging overhead, and I don't think I am ready for the storm that is about to hit.

Afterglow showed up for a meeting with Fly By only minutes ago, and for that whole time I have stood here paralysed. She hasn't even looked at me for more than a second. I don't know how I feel about that. I should be relieved…right? So why aren't I?

Reckless Tunez put the gathering on today because our tour starts next week, and they wanted to ensure we all knew each other. We will be living in close contact for the whole tour—which is going to be broken up and take a year, two if everything gets organised for the European and Asian countries—and they don't want any drama that can leak to the tabloids and cause negative press.

Fly By and Afterglow. A rock band and a county band lined up together to travel in close confines together from next Monday. A week is all I have left before being stuck with her until who knows when. Being in her presence now is both revealing and torturous.

Ali's voice rings through the room, jolting me.

How am I going to survive this?

Two - Alintia

I CANNOT BELIEVE I am in the almost holy presence of Fly By. They are Rock Gods and changed modern music as we know it. When I got the call telling me I was going to be their opening act on this tour, I almost fainted. It was one thing to be called by Reckless Tunez and be offered a contract. It was a completely different thing to be entrusted with being Fly By's opening act.

Signing with Reckless Tunez has been the real starting point of my career. Up until then, I wasn't sure when—or if—I would ever break into the music industry, especially because I don't have anything to offer except my voice. It is my blessing and my curse—I can sing with no hesitation, can carry almost any tune I hear, but I have no talent in the way of playing an instrument. Regardless of what instrument I try, it always sounds like nails on a chalkboard—screechy and all wrong.

The day I received the call from Reckless Tunez asking me to come in, my whole life changed.

Running to their studio was not a good idea. My hair is in knots, I am out of breath and I can feel sweat dripping down my back—but what else was supposed to do to get to their office so quickly? I had taken the bus as far as it would get me and had to get out and walk the rest of the way. Or I should say run.

I pat my hair down, huffing and puffing trying to calm down my breathing and cool down all at once—not that it is helping much. I am on the verge of hyperventilating. A few more seconds, then I will go in.

The door to the studio offices open, and a man exits, making a beeline straight for me.

"Ali?" his deep voice rumbles. His voice is exquisite—he would be a great audiobook narrator.

"Y-Yes," I pant slightly as my breathing slowly returns to normal.

"Mitch." He extends his hand, and I offer mine in return, shaking his hand. "Did you want to come inside so we can have a chat?"

"Yes, sorry, I was just about to head in." I offer a weak smile.

"Great, is your agent meeting you here?" Mitch asks as I follow him through the doors.

"I—ah, I don't have one. Is that going to be a problem?"

"No, it's all good. We can just go over everything today, and if you would like you can get a lawyer to look over everything before you sign."

Lawyer? Agent? I know they called me to come in, but they must actually be serious about signing me if they are already talking contracts!

"Ok. That sounds good." I saw this lobby before when I dropped in my demo, but now I feel like I am looking at it with new eyes.

The floor is covered in a plush beige carpet. A walnut reception desk stands about a metre tall and displays glass awards, flowers, and has a small bowl of candy. The walls are off-white and covered in music tour posters, platinum and diamond record keepsakes. Mitch leads me past the smiling receptionist and into a small board room, the décor and colour scheme matching reception.

"Did you want a coffee or water?" he asks me.

"Just a water is fine, thank you." I hesitate awkwardly in the room, standing just inside the door. Mitch ducks his head out and calls out to the receptionist for two waters before closing the door behind him, effectively trapping me in there with him.

"Please Ali, have a seat." Mitch indicates the swivel chairs surrounding the walnut meeting table and I gratefully sit down. My throat is all dried up, and my nerves are on the edge of their seat. Tense with whatever this meeting could accomplish for me.

"Ali, I want to get straight to the point so there isn't any confusion, ok?" I nod. He smiles and continues, "Reckless Tunez would like to offer you a contract. We have a few ideas for what direction we can take you in, but I think we can assemble a good team and band that suits you. We would start off small. A single or two, and see how they trend in the charts before considering albums, etc."

On the inside I am that gif from Seinfeld—hands in the air, happy dancing. On the outside, I am trying so hard not to actually get up and do that. A smile breaks across my face.

"You're serious?" I laugh nervously.

"Yes, Ali, we are."

Glancing around the meeting room, I feel the same excitement I had eight months ago—except this time I am not meeting my band for the first time. I am meeting Fly By for the first time. Only last week Mitch told me that Afterglow had been booked in to be the opening act for the Fly By tour. I found out we were with the same label about a month after I signed my contract, when I met Joel. Mitch introduced us when Joel came into the studio one day. I didn't even know Reckless managed Fly By, but I was stunned when he came into the room and I instantly recognised him as Joel from Fly By. Since then I haven't seen Joel, met the rest of the band, or seen them together. I suppose they have their own recording studios and don't need to come here, or maybe we have just never been here at the same time.

My eyes dart around the room to Maverick, the oldest brother and lead guitarist, who has shaggy brown hair just coming to his shoulders, next to his new girlfriend Cecilia. With her fiery red hair, part of her face is obscured with dark sunglasses, and a white cane is held at her side—they were in the media a few months ago when she snatched up the bad boy fan-favourite bachelor. I see Joel, long brown hair pulled up into a man-bun, a gorgeous thick beard almost brushing his collar bone—I have to resist walking up to him and burying my fingers in it—*stop Ali!*

Charlie next to him is his equal in good looks, but even as his identical twin, his beard is kept to a three-day growth and his hair shorter. Tom is clean-shaven with shaggy long hair and has brighter clothing than his brothers, a pastel green t-shirt and washed-out jeans. Ethan is also clean-shaven, hair cropped relatively short with a long-on-top style, wearing black distressed denim shorts and a t-shirt with the Fly By logo on it.

From just looking at them you can see they are all related. Same colouring, same eyes, only varying slightly in shades of hazel with yellow and green. They are even similar in height and build, about six feet. They are all in good…no, great shape. Muscles and tattoos on display everywhere. I mentally shake myself out of staring and wipe the drool off my face before stepping further into the room. The rest of my band files in behind me as Mitch makes introductions.

"Fly By, meet your opening act, Afterglow," Mitch says, gesturing to us. "This is Ali Hawkins, lead singer and front woman. Jax Tomas, who's on bass, Stephanie Anderson on guitar, and Chris Jonson on drums. Afterglow," Mitch continues. He introduces each of the guys, and then introduced Cecilia. "She also works for Reckless Tunez and will gradually transition to being your direct manager instead of me."

I am a bit overwhelmed—seeing them all in the flesh. Even though I have never been a huge fan, you have to be ignorant to have no idea who the Fly By boys are. I feel eyes on me and glance around to see Joel glaring at me. If his eyes were a death ray, I would have died minutes ago. He didn't look at me like this the first time I met him. What has brought this on? I haven't even said anything yet…should I have said something already? Shit!

"Hi!" I squeak. *Waaay too eager there, Ali.* I clear my throat. "It's nice to meet you all. I am looking forward to the tour and getting to open for you guys! This is such an amazing opportunity!"

"Yeah, well, it's not like we had any say in the matter," Joel grumbles, finally taking his heavy gaze off me as he walks over to a table of snacks and drinks.

"Joel!" Maverick scolds him.

"What? It's the truth. They were thrust upon us because they are the *next big thing*," Joel says, his words dripping with venom. "They are just using us to get more famous—just like everyone else." He grabs a bottle of Coke from the table and saunters out of the room.

Woah.

"Please excuse Joel," Charlie says, addressing me and my band. "He hasn't been himself lately. Even I don't know what is going on with him." He mumbled the last part, not intending for anyone other than his brothers to hear him, probably.

"I'll go speak with him," Tom says, stepping out of the room to follow his brother.

We stand all stand there, tense. I have no idea how to move on from this. My bandmates gravitate towards the table of refreshments and, with nothing better to do, I follow them. Tentative conversation breaks out between the two bands. Ethan is clearly flirting with Steph, while Charlie and Maverick talk to Jax and Chris. With a bottle of water in my hand, I manoeuvre myself to stand next to Cecilia.

"So, manager," I begin nervously, "how do you feel about working with us instead of Fly By?"

"It will be good, I think," Cecilia replies softly. "I will still be on tour with Maverick and the guys, but I won't be distracted by him during working hours—and I have always wanted to be an agent or producer, and this is a step in that direction. Maverick has let me into his song writing process, too. Nothing is more fascinating than sitting there listening to him construct a song from nothing."

"I am glad you guys can make it work, and I am looking forward to the tour and working with you."

"I am too. I honestly wasn't sure where my career in music would lead once I finished university a few months ago. But crashing into Maverick was definitely the best thing that has ever happened to me."

"Crashing into Maverick?"

"Oh, don't tell me you don't know the story?"

"I'm sorry, but I haven't an idea what you are talking about. I have only seen what was in the tabloids, and I do my best to avoid them knowing how factual they can be."

"Ah, well let me enlighten you then. One day Maverick wasn't looking where he was going—it really was his fault as he doesn't have the excuse of being blind like I do—and bowled into me. Both of us fall to the floor, I lost my cane and broke my laptop."

"Oh no!" I exclaim.

"Yeah, I was pretty devastated. Mav took care of everything though. And here we are." Her smile is radiant, full of love and fondness for her boyfriend—I long to have someone look like that when they think about me.

After about an hour, Tom rejoined the group with a reluctant looking Joel. Tom quickly intermingled with the bands, joining a conversation that Jax was having with Cecilia and I about what to expect on tour. I watch Joel stalk to the far side of the room, sitting down in a chair and—for lack of a better word —sulking. What is his problem? How can someone hate our band so much without even meeting us? It's not like we asked to be their opening act. And did he have to be so attractive? Couldn't he be as ugly as his behaviour? That would make it easier to stop staring at him.

I hadn't thought of a man like this for months. I was so caught up in creating the band, establishing that relationship and creating an album, I had no time to even think about dating.

I had never had luck in love anyway. The guy Chloe set me up with never did show up and I have no idea what happened to that great guy I accidentally hit it off with. The memory of him was overshadowed by the record deal with Reckless, and even though I can remember our connection, and the colour of his shoes, the picture of him has warped over time. Occasionally he pops into my mind, and I wonder where he is and what he thought about me—the random woman who just insisted he was on a date with her. It's not like I really gave him a chance to explain he wasn't who I thought he was.

Joel meets my gaze, and I quickly look away, my cheeks heating with embarrassment at being caught staring.

I wonder if I will ever find Starbucks man again.

3

Three - Joel

SITTING IN THE EMPTY SEATS, I feel like a scolded child. My brothers have been on my case for the last few weeks. They don't understand why I have been so out of it, and unable to "give Afterglow a chance." My brothers should have my side—isn't that the way things are meant to be? Family before all else?

I suppose they would be on my side if they understood what happened, but I cannot bring myself to tell them. What if they take her side? All I know is I cannot be near her. I don't trust myself to not fawn all over her again, embarrassing myself and just getting rejected again. Sitting here now, I am stuck suffering through watching her and her band practice and do a final system check.

We already had our practice earlier and I had tried to leave straight afterwards, planning to avoid watching Afterglow practice like I have every time we have had joint sessions in the lead up to the tour. Unfortunately for me, Mitch stopped me before I could leave—I have to stay since there is another party tonight that both bands need to attend. You would think after the failure that was our initial band introduction that they wouldn't want me to be there.

I force myself to look at my phone while Ali is preforming up on stage. She wasn't wrong when she said she could sing anything. Her voice is angelic, jolting through me when she hits note after note—and I know if I watch her, I'll be caught out and everyone will see the hearts in my eyes. Scrolling through my phone doesn't help at all. My social media is covered with promos for the new tour, fans shipping Ali and Charlie together—like why Charlie? How is he a better fit for her than I am?

Not the point! I mentally scold myself.

I stumbled across Alintia's Instagram a few months ago when we were both tagged in a post from Reckless. As hard as I tried to resist—I have been low-key stalking her since. I don't follow her, so I don't see everything she posts, but every so often I will go onto her page and scroll through her photos. Her most recent post fills my screen. **"Getting ready to go on tour with @FlyByBoys for the next few weeks, but can't leave without a goodbye to my family! @NaomiandMarley @chloe4sure."** With a huge grin, Ali sits in the centre of the photograph, her mum, Naomi, her dad, and Marley are sitting either side of her, arms wrapped around Ali. She has her dad's smile, and her mum's eyes. Chloe, Ali's best friend and who set her up on the blind date, is lying across their laps on her side. Her head is resting on her arm in Naomi's lap.

This small insight into her life makes me feel like I can see the real Alintia, who is involved with her community and loves her family. Yet I do not know anything that really matters when it comes to Alintia.

The practice wraps up, and we are led out of the practice hall and out to a line of black Audi SUVs. They have been organised to chauffeur us all around while we are in Queensland, and we will have something similar in all the cities we fly to over the next few weeks. According to Mitch, they are the best for anonymity. I am not sure about that. Surely, we would blend in more with a Toyota Camry or Holden Commodore —from my experience, those are two of the most common cars in Australia.

Eager to get the hell out of here and get this party over and done with, I shuffle along to the last car in the line-up and hop into the back seat. I stare out the window, my eyes not focusing on anything as I listen to everyone else chatter and move about organising themselves into cars. I don't turn as the car seat shifts, alerting me to someone sitting next to me, a soft floral scent now filling the car. Is it too much to hope that it is Steph who has sought me out? Keeping my face turned away, a soft hand touches my forearm, resting against my knee. I jolt at the soft touch, whipping my head around and staring into wide electric blue eyes—closer than she has ever been before. Of course, I am not lucky enough for it to not be *her*.

Within seconds my mind registers that we are alone in the backseat of this SUV. Only the driver and security guard are in the front seat, paying us no attention as we roll through the city streets.

"I'm sorry," Ali says gently. "I didn't mean to startle you."

"Um," I clear my throat, "it's fine. Whatever."

I tear my gaze from her, scooting over in my seat to be as far from her as possible and looking back out the window.

"Are you ok?" She asks.

"I'm fine," I manage to get out gruffly.

"I only ask as your brothers say you have been different lately. I wasn't sure if it was something you could talk to them about. Is there any way I can help? I won't judge you at all."

Of course. Of course, she is sweet and caring.

It occurs to me then that her hand is still on my arm, my skin burning up at her touch. I yank my arm away and turn back to the window.

This car trip—this tour—cannot be over soon enough.

"Jack and Coke please," I say to the bartender.

The moment I entered the party, I found the bar and started looking for a human shield for the night. The car trip with her was painful enough. I don't need to spend the rest of the night forced to be civil with her. Being in the same vicinity as her has just confirmed what I have been trying to ignore—I am still drawn to her, and I hate her for it. I still crave her touch, her taste—fuck, I would be happy with just speaking with her again like we did that day in Starbucks. She shouldn't have this kind of hold over me, which tells me I really need to keep my distance from her. The party is being hosted by Reckless Tunez, and in attendance are other musicians, celebrities, and a few fans that I'm assuming won tickets to be here on some radio show.

As the bartender hands me my drink, a petite woman squishes into the non-existent space between me and another guest at the bar, pressing her enhanced chest against my arm. I look her over out of the corner of my eye. Her bleach blonde hair cascades over one shoulder, leaving the other one bare in her strapless, bright red cocktail dress. A year ago, I would've been eager to have her attention—and do what she is clearly wanting. Now, there is a certain chocolate-skinned beauty that my cock thinks is the be-all-end-all. He has no interest in anyone else.

"Hello, Joel. I am Zoe, it's nice to meet you," she says seductively.

Taking a large gulp of my drink, I turn to face her fully.

"Hi, Zoe. What brings you here today?"

"My friend works here and managed to sneak me in. I just had to meet you," she gushes, placing a tentative hand against my chest.

"Oh really?" A super fan, those are always fun. Zoe isn't exactly my type, but she would be a good distraction from Ali for the night. "Can I get you a drink?"

Zoe nods enthusiastically as I flag the bartender down.

"Another Jack and Coke please and whatever this fine lady would like," I say, gesturing for Zoe to order.

"A fruit-tingle please."

"Sure," the bartender replies, walking away to get our drinks.

"So, tell me a bit about you, Zoe."

I catch Ali's gaze over Zoe's shoulder, standing across the room surrounded by my brothers and other industry executives. Getting the royal treatment. I have to stop myself from scoffing and tune back into Zoe realising that I haven't heard a word she said—too focused on Ali, again.

"So, are you looking forward to the tour?" Zoe asks me.

No, I am dreading it—all thanks to a certain singer! Thanks for the reminder, I want to say, but I can't. I don't know Zoe from a bar of soap, and I know that most people won't hesitate to take any sound bite or quote they can to the tabloids.

"Yeah," I reply using my interview voice, "it's gonna be great. I am looking forward to Afterglow opening for us. Have you heard their work?"

"Bits and pieces, but they aren't as great as Fly By is," Zoe says, pushing up against me again—making it very evident she would be down for anything with me tonight.

"Ugh, finally!" Zoe says as the bartender returns with our drinks. She picks up the blue and purple concoction, playing with the straw against her mouth, her tongue darting out every so often to lick the air next to the straw…is that meant to be sexy? Cause it really isn't. She looks like someone who is trying to catch the straw with their mouth and keeps missing —you know that scene in movies where the dude is too distracted by the TV to get his straw in his mouth? It's kinda odd, actually.

I take a step away from the bar, opting to be somewhere not so crowded. As expected, Zoe follows me. We take up a spot at a small cocktail table against the wall, and thankfully Zoe stands across the table, freeing up my personal space. Unfortunately, this angle isn't any better. I can still see Ali—centre of attention, and now not paying me any attention. What does she make of all this, I wonder?

No! I am not spending time thinking about her anymore!

The rest of the night passes quickly. Zoe follows me around like a bad smell, and I can't hate it. It's nice to feel wanted by a woman after being used and discarded by Ali. It's also the perfect excuse for my brothers to leave me alone—if they think I have a chance to get laid tonight, they won't interfere. They might even encourage it if they think that's what my issue is.

I wonder what they would think about how long it's been since I have had sex. I haven't been abstaining on purpose—I just haven't wanted to fuck anyone since I met Ali. How fucked is that? Maybe I should fuck Zoe—start the healing process and move on from Ali.

But I know I won't.

That's why I am screwed.

Four - Alintia

THE CROWD'S roar can be heard all the way in our dressing room. I know their excitement isn't for us exactly, but I am still caught up in the hype. This is our first concert on tour. Our first concert in front of an audience of this size. And it is starting to hit me just how crazy this is.

Out there, there is roughly ten thousand people who I am going to have to sing and perform in front of in only—I check the clock—fifteen minutes.

Shit.

"I need the bathroom," I blurt out, practically running out of the dressing room.

Nausea churns through me. I need to find a private toilet before I embarrass myself in front of everyone. Rushing down the hallway, I dodge sound technicians and the setup crew before finally crashing through the bathroom door.

Chest heaving as I try to catch my breath, I screech to a stop at the sight of Joel in the bathroom—his wide back to me as he relieves himself in the toilet.

"Uh…" I fumble, reaching behind me for the door but only grasping air.

"Can I help you with something?" Joel asks dismissively, slowly zipping up his jeans and turning to face me.

I am unable to meet his eyes, my focus solely on his bare chest and the tattoos on full display.

"I…uh…huh?" I manage to get out while my mind is still reeling—going from panic to whatever this is in seconds has confused my brain.

"What are you doing here?" his rough voice echoes off the tiles.

"What are you going here?" I ask, tearing my eyes away from his chest at last.

"Taking a piss. What did it look like? Now you?"

"I…uh…" I had nothing—nothing except the truth. "I was coming here to throw up. I started thinking about the audience size and the show and I just panicked." My heart is beating so fast, it feels like it will burst out of my chest.

"Don't you have a bathroom off of your dressing rooms?" he asks mildly.

"Yeah, but I didn't want the others to know that I was nervous. I am their leader—you know?" I babble, no longer in control of my mouth. "Like—I have to keep up appearances. They can't see me as a wreck. I need to hold them together. Which doesn't make sense why I would tell you all this. You'll just bitch about me to everyone anyway." I turn away, again reaching out for the door handle—clasping it in my hand this time.

"Wait," Joel says softly. I hesitate, but don't turn around. "Our first show this big—it was insane. Probably six months after we won *What It Takes!*, we were in the middle of the US and I remember being told that we had sold out all the seats in the venue. I was torn between being elated and being shit scared. I get what you mean about needing to keep it together for the rest of the band."

His deep voice bounces of the tiles, wrapping around me—warming me and sending shivers down my spine.

"Even though we don't really have a leader, per se," he goes on, "I had to keep myself in check for my younger brothers, to lead by examplc and be strong for them in case they needed to freak out. We thought we had all gotten over stage fright by then, but that show really took us to the next level. So I get it. I'll get out of your way so you can use the toilet and get on stage. You'll do a great job, Alintia."

Joel says all this to my back, and when I finally turn around, I see him exiting through a second door I hadn't noticed. Was this his private bathroom?

I walk to the basin, wetting a paper towel and moving it to the back of my neck, staring at myself in the mirror. All my panic has dried up—comforted, and dissolved by Joel's story. Maybe we do have something in common after all.

"Afterglow, five minutes to show time; please report to the stage," a muffled voice comes through the bathroom door.

No time left then. I discard the paper towel and check that I look put together before exiting the bathroom.

When I get to the stage, I quickly pull out my phone, taking a photo of the stage from the wings and sending the photo in a mass text to my parents, Chloe, my aunts, uncles, and cousins.

Me: *Squee! * You ready for this?

This is something I do for all my gigs, even when—like tonight —they are all in the crowd. With settled nerves, I step onto the stage with only one lingering thought floating around in my mind: Why wasn't Joel an asshole?

Joel

I shouldn't be here. I should be with my brothers or in my dressing room doing last-minute vocal warm-ups. I should be doing anything other than standing in the shadows on the wings of the stage watching Alintia on stage. I told the sound technicians I am only watching to ensure that they won't fuck up our reputation—thankfully they left me in peace as I was out of their way. I think they are too intimidated by me to question the obvious lie.

I wasn't expecting her to burst into my bathroom minutes before she was due on stage—her eyes wide with panic, her normally brown complexion pale, visible even through her heavy stage makeup. I shouldn't have spoken to her, and I had no place doing that—just like I had no place in standing here watching her show now. What was I thinking?

I need to put even more walls up between us if I am still letting myself be manipulated. Shaking my head, I turn away from the stage, starting the walk back to my dressing room. I can't indulge in this any longer. She rejected me. I need to move on and get over it—otherwise the next few months will be the death of me.

Ali's soft voice rings through the concert hall, chasing me as I walk through the twisted hallways, dodging everyone rushing around backstage. The allure of her voice nips at my heels, a siren's call beckoning me to return to her, put her in her place, and claim her for myself.

Needing a distraction, I head to Charlie's dressing room. When we first started out with concerts like this, we were all huddled into one room, cramped together trying to change and warm up. Nowadays, our venues are big enough for us all to have our own rooms—not that we don't regularly go to each other's now.

"Come in," Charlie calls out after I knock on his door.

"Hey, man. How are you doing?" I ask him, entering the room and flopping down onto the couch next to him.

"I'm good, bro. What's up?"

"Nothing, just bored," I reply lamely.

"Ha! No you aren't. Seriously, what's up? You have been acting weird for weeks."

"Char—"

"No," he cuts me off, "I know we all like to keep our secrets, but you and I normally tell each other everything. What is going on with you?"

A heavy sigh escapes me and I sink further into the couch. "I have met Ali—before all this tour shit started, I mean. A couple months ago, I guess you could call it a date. She was meant to have a blind date and got me confused with the guy she was meant to meet."

"Ok…I am not seeing an issue here?"

"Dude, do we really need to go over this?" I complain.

"Yes, clearly we do, cause whatever 'this' is has you fucked up."

"She has me twisted up, ok?" I blurt out, pushing myself to my feet. I start pacing, frustrated we are even needing to have a conversation. "I was captivated by her and she had me fooled. She ran off before I could get anything more than her name…a few weeks later she was all over the media. I met her in the studio and she recognised me on sight. The first words out of her mouth were *'Oh my god! It's you!'* and I thought maybe…maybe we had a chance to finish that date. Until she started gushing about Fly By—and our fame—like a groupie. It made me feel like she's manipulated me to benefit her. Maybe that day in Starbucks she knew who I was and played along, trying to date me in the hopes of using my connections if her demos didn't work out. The second she got a phone call from Reckless, she was out the door without a look back at me. Then with this tour, when we met up, she acted like she had never met me before." As shit as it is, it feels good to get all of this off my chest. I hate keeping things from my brothers, especially my twin.

"Did you talk to her about it?" Charlie asks.

I halt my pacing, turning to face him as I sag against the wall. "I tried when we were in the car together the other day…she all but confirmed that I was recognisable and that she had always known who I was." I feel pathetic. Moping over a woman who clearly doesn't care about me.

"I'm sorry, J," Charlie soothes, standing and crossing over to me.

"It's whatever. It's just being this close to her is getting to me. I am all twisted up still wanting her and I can't get over it while being in such close contact."

"I am sure over time you will get past it. I can see now why you have been a dick."

"Hey! I wasn't a dick!" I protest, glaring at him.

"Yeah, you were. But I get it. I know what it's like to see a person you want to be with and not being able to touch or love them the way you want to," Charlie says, his voice ringing with longing and hopelessness.

And yeah, Charlie would know that feeling.

Five - Alintia

SURE, I have performed on stage and done concerts before. But nothing could compare to what I just experienced.

Ten thousand people. I just sang my heart out in front of ten thousand people. Once I grasped my microphone, all my nerves faded and it was just another chance to sing, to share my voice and songs with the world around me.

I knew that most of the patrons were here for Fly By, but I heard some of them singing along to our songs—calling out over the music for their favourite songs and screaming out the lyrics. I don't think anything can compare to this feeling.

I am still on a high hours later, too on edge to sit down, and linger as we all gather together in the green room for the after-party. The VIP ticket holders are here too, having just finished their meet and greets with the boys of Fly By, and food and drinks are being carried around by waiters hired for the event. I am bouncing on the balls of my toes, sipping on a water to keep myself hydrated, watching the group around me unfold.

My family and Chloe had stopped by after the show with the backstage passes by Reckless for the opening night show. It was otherworldly, taking my family through the backstage areas and our dressing room, showing them what is, essentially, my new life. They left a few hours ago now, and Chloe stayed to keep me company—but she is now in a deep conversation with my guitarist, Steph. They have met once or twice since we were all paired up together and seem to get along well.

I gravitate towards Cecilia, hoping I can pick up a conversation with her like the last gathering we had, but before I can reach her, I see Maverick wrap his arm around her and sweep her into an aggressively passionate kiss.

What is it like, I wonder, to experience that sort of passion and love for someone? I have never felt like that. My mind flicks back to Jay like it so often has over the last year. Maybe he would have been that for me. I guess I will never know.

I lean against the wall, watching the crowd around me. Jax and Chris are mingling with some of the VIPs and sound techs that were invited to this wrap party.

Movement catches the corner of my eye. I turn to see Joel— who has managed to lose his shirt and has a woman on each arm. It irks me to note both of them are almost polar opposites of me. One is blonde, the other's hair is a cobalt blue, their skin glistening a slight orange from fake tans. An unexplainable jolt of anger goes through me, twisting my face into a scowl, as he leans in to kiss the blonde full on the mouth. I can see tongues battling each other. The hand he had wrapped around her waist drops to palm her ass cheek. All while the other watches on, longing all over her face until he turns and gives her the same treatment.

I scoff, turning away from the sight only to meet Charlie's accusing gaze. What the fuck did I do to piss him off? I thought it was only Joel who irrationally hated me. Now I have to deal with the other brothers getting on my case too?

Whatever.

I am here to finally live my dream and do my job—I am not here to fall in love with a rock star. No matter how hot, sweet at times, and confusing Joel can be. No matter what pull I have to him—there is no point in getting caught up in whatever game the brothers are playing.

"Hey Ali," Mitch says, breaking into my runaway thoughts.

"Mitch, what's up?" I ask.

"Good. What's with the scowl?" Mitch asks, following to where my gaze had lingered for so long. Watching as Joel is now doing tequila shots; licking the salt off blonde's neck and getting the lemon from her cleavage. "Ah, just ignore the boys. Rock star life—you'll get it one day. Come and meet Travis. He is the producer who did that new single of Madison Dai's that's currently a top 10 on the ARIA charts."

Diligently, I follow Mitch through to the adjoining room, meeting industry professionals and networking within an inch of my life—I don't know how long we will be lucky enough to keep our deal with Reckless Tunez, but now that I have my foot in the industry door, I will do whatever it takes to stay here.

It's like Joel is following me around the after party. Every time I turn my head, he is there with those two girls hanging off his arms. Why doesn't he just leave already? It's obvious that they are eager to have sex with him, whatever way they can get it. I turn away disgusted and find myself face to face with Charlie, again.

"Oh, hey," I say, shock coursing through me from his proximity.

"Hi, Ali. How was your first concert?" Charlie asks. His voice —his face, everything really—is so similar to Joel's. I knew they were identical twins, but seriously—even their voices are the same?

"Can you sing like him too?" I ask before my mind can catch up with my mouth.

"What?" Charlie asks, amusement curling his lips into a soft grin.

"Uh, you and Joel are identical…right?"

"Yes, that's obvious—isn't it?"

"Yeah, so I was wondering, can you sing like him too? Or is that unique to him?"

"Ah…that's just Joel. He has a talent for it—while I can sing and carry a tune, it's nothing like what J can do."

"Mmm." I find my eyes on Joel again. He is sitting down now, both women sitting on his lap, claiming a leg each as they fawn all over him.

A stab of jealousy blooms in my chest. What the fuck is that? Why would I be jealous…? It's not like I want to be sitting on his lap, being the sole recipient of his attention as he licks my neck to do a shot, grinding his erection into my ass while no one else would be able to see it.

Oh my gosh. I want Joel. Asshole, standoffish, sweet, womaniser Joel.

Fuck my life.

Disgust roils through me.

"What's wrong?" Charlie asks, studying my face intensely.

"Nothing, I just don't get why he doesn't take them back to his room already. It's not like we need to see that shit."

"Why does it bother you?" he asks, still staring at me like a bug under a microscope.

"It's just inappropriate. That…that should be done behind closed doors."

"So, it's not that it's not you?"

I whip my head around to stare at Charlie, forcing my face to remain neutral.

"He can do whatever—and whoever—he wants. I don't give a shit," I protest way too strongly.

Thankfully, Charlie doesn't call me on it. He just gives me a look that I cannot decipher before I leave to find Mitch again. Is it too soon for me to return to the hotel and get this long ass night over and done with?

6

Six - Joel

MY HEAD ACHES–A pounding shaking through my whole body. All I want to do is crawl up in a ball and die.

We have had five shows on tour so far, one week down—and it hasn't been too bad. Except I'm trying to avoid Ali at every step, and if I can't, sometimes all I can do is drink until I forget she's in the same room.

"Tequila, eh?" Ethan yells at me.

Well maybe he is just talking normally, but with this hangover it may as well be an amplifier right inside my skull.

"Shut up!" I grumble, huddling over myself as I lean against the bus window. Thankfully today is just a travel day.

Ethan chuckles, clearly having no pity for me or my condition. We are in the coach bus that Reckless had organised to transport us around Queensland, and I have the misfortune of having Ethan sitting directly in front of me.

When we have several shows in the same state, we will probably have a similar setup—but we thankfully are flying between the major cities. I don't think I could manage being in a cramped bus for more than twenty hours—let alone being surrounded by my brothers, Afterglow, and all the hangers-on.

"Leave me alone," I complain, my throat hoarse after spending half the night throwing up. I shift in my seat to face Ethan. Oh. The pounding in my head wasn't just the tequila, it was the vibration of the bus.

Why are we here again? Why did I drink so much?

"Here, this might help," a melodic voice says. There is only one person in this world whose voice sounds like that.

Ali.

I glance over the empty seat next to me and see Ali standing there with a bottle of water, a banana, and a packet of Panadol.

I want to turn her down. I don't need her pity or her to care for me. My stomach churns and I know that I need the items she has.

"Thanks," I grunt, causing my throat to flare in pain. Stupid move. I need to heal. I need to sing tomorrow night.

This is the first words she has been able to speak to me since opening night.

I unscrew the water cap, drinking almost half the bottle before I pop two tablets in my mouth. Once I have those down, I peel and eat the banana. I suddenly imagine her putting it between her lips, and just the thought of seeing anything phallic near Ali's mouth has my cock twitching.

Thankfully, the Panadol starts to kick in, taking the edge off my hangover. We had another after-party last night and I may have done one too many shots.

Normally I know my limit. I know how many drinks I can have to have a good time but not wake up with a hangover. Except last night Ali was there, and she was flirting with one of the producers. And instead of taking my frustrations out on a willing hot piece of ass—I drank most of a bottle of tequila.

For some fucked up reason, I haven't had sex with anyone in months. I tried the first night on tour—I really thought I could move on and spend my night with two hot chicks. When the party was over, they were more than ready to accompany me to my hotel room—or the nearest private space that I would be willing to fuck them in. My cock had no interest. The traitor.

I dumped those chicks at security with some bullshit excuse and went up to my room alone. My mind had wandered to Ali, and my traitorous dick suddenly had life again. In my drunken haze, I jerked off to thoughts of Ali in all sorts of positions.

Since then, it's like that part of my mind has been unlocked and next to everything she does turns me on. How can I possibly still be feeling this way?

I am so fucked.

I doze in and out for the rest of the bus trip, waking up enough to get assigned a hotel room, bustle my way into it, and collapse face first into the king-size bed—falling into a dreamless sleep.

When I come to, it's been a few hours and thankfully the last of my hangover has disappeared. I really need to consider how much I drink going forward. I place a call to room service for what sounds like a nice pasta dish and sit back on the couch while scrolling through my phone, catching up on everything I missed while I was dead to the world.

A restless feeling overwhelms me after I finish eating, no doubt in thanks to spending most of the day asleep. I glance at the clock. It's almost midnight and I am wide awake. When we are on tour, we are nearly always surrounded by security guards. However, in this hotel, our floor requires a special key to access it, so there are only two guards on duty down in the lobby.

I leave my room and pace the hallway, but it's not enough. I need to be more active. I can basically feel my skin itching with the need to do something—anything—to burn up all this energy. I know I shouldn't, but it doesn't stop me. What's the worst that could happen at this time of night?

I call the elevator and cross my fingers that there are no guards loitering inside. When the doors open, it is blissfully empty. Good. I won't have to explain this adventure to anyone. We are on the penthouse level, and I take the elevator all the way down to the first level where the hotel gym and pool is. I thought about going for a run on the treadmill, but I am not wearing the right shoes for that. Instead, I enter the pool area, which is also deserted. I am pretty sure it's meant to be shut at this time, but I am not going to complain that the staff are running late tonight. It's only a small pool—about twenty-five meters long and only three meters wide. It's not what I am used to, but it will do for getting some laps in.

I strip down to my briefs, leaving my jeans, shirt, and shoes in a pile on one of the loungers, and drive right into the deep end. The itching feeling subsides as I move through the water, slicing through it with sharp movements. When I finally start to tire, I pull myself up to sit on the side of the pool, my breath slightly laboured from the intense workout. I strip off my wet underwear and, wrapping a towel around my waist, I gather all my clothes in one hand and make my way back to my bedroom.

The clock in the elevator tells me it is now one thirty in the morning. Hopefully, when I get back to my room, I can get a couple more hours of sleep in without fucking up my sleep schedule.

As I step out of the elevator, I hear a soft strumming. It must be Maverick. He has been known to burn the midnight oil writing at all hours of the night. I follow the sound down the hallway and find a meeting room—that is also for our exclusive use—with its door propped open. As I take a step into the room, she starts singing, and my steps falter. It's not Maverick.

It's Alintia.

Why is it always Alintia—it's like she is everywhere I go now. My body is rooted in place, unable to do anything as my eyes fall on her and my heart rate starts to speed up again.

She is sitting on the carpet pressed up next to the floor-to-ceiling windows. Outside are only the colourful city lights, the moon, and as many stars as you can see in a city. Ali is wearing an emerald-green silk nightgown. Spaghetti straps leave her shoulders and arms bare. A small stereo sits next to her, and I realise that is where the strumming is coming from. She is barefoot and her hair falls in her natural messy ringlets, skimming over her shoulder blades as she sings her heart out to the city below her. I haven't seen her natural hair since our

Starbucks date—it has always been straightened and styled on stage.

I had thought she was beautiful before. My image of her has nothing on this raw, complete version of herself.

"Joel, fuck!" Ali jolts, finally noticing my reflection in the window.

She scrambles to her feet as I just stand there like an idiot. In her rush to stand, one of the straps of her nightgown falls off her shoulder, showing me more of her beautiful brown skin. The slip of the gown shifts, baring the top of her full breasts. I stare at her chest, captivated as her chest heaves, sending her tits bouncing—unrestrained. I want nothing more than to hold those boobs in my hands, my fingers tweaking her nipples as my tongue invades her mouth. My cock hardens, reminding me that I am naked under my towel, staring at her.

"Uh, sorry," I manage to say. "I heard the music and thought you were Maverick. Sorry. I shouldn't have disturbed you." I step backwards, now desperate to get out of this room before she can push this any further.

"Why don't you like me?" Ali asks so softly I can barely hear her across the room.

"What?" I ask, my eyes narrowed on hers.

"You don't like me—never have from the day we met. Why?"

"Oh, I liked you the day we met," I confess before I can think it through. "I was wrapped around your little finger, until I realised exactly who you are, *Ali*," I seethe, my anger over taking me.

"I don't understand," she replies innocently.

"I am not falling for that act again."

"What act? I don't know what you are talking about!" Ali yells back at me, her bare feet thudding against the carpeted floor as she stalks over to me. I had never noticed just how short she was compared to me. How could I? The first time we met, we were both sitting down, and she has always been in heels every time I have seen her. The top of her head would barely hit my chin, if at all. She tilts her head to glare at me and slaps her palms against my bare chest. "What the *fuck* is your problem, Joel?" she growls in my face.

I try to stop myself. I really do. But my body is no longer attached to my brain apparently.

"You're my problem, Alintia," I growl.

Within seconds I drop my clothes, abandoning the towel as my right hand wraps around both of her wrists, showing just how small she is compared to me. I meet her gaze—those vivid blue eyes full of heat and anger. My left hand cups her jaw, holding her head in place as I crash my mouth down on hers.

Electric tingles shoot throughout my whole body as my lips cover hers. I could get high off this feeling. Die right now and be okay with it because I got to feel this way just once in my life.

Ali pulls back, breaking the kiss and yanking herself out of my grip.

"What the fuck was that?" she pants.

"I—I—" I stammer out. I don't even know how to answer her.

Ali glares at me for a minute, seeming to realise that I am not going to answer her. She brushes past me and storms out of the room. Seconds later I hear the beep of her room door.

Leaving me standing here naked, with the sweet taste of her lips on my tongue.

And a raging boner.

Seven - Alintia

IT'S BEEN a week since that moonlit kiss with Joel and I still don't know what to make of it. I shouldn't have stormed out, but I didn't know what else to do. I thought maybe it might have been a changing point in our relationship. I walked into the tour bus the next day hopeful that he might want to talk about it—not that I knew what to say. Nothing changed though; he ignored me just as he has every day since the tour began. That hurt me more than I was expecting it to.

Today is another travel day, so after getting off the plane, I settle into the hotel room I am sharing with Steph in Melbourne, waiting around for the team meeting later. Over the last two weeks, we have had concerts in the Gold Coast, Brisbane, Maroochydore, Newcastle, Sydney, and Wollongong. This is the most I have travelled in my life, and the furthest I have been from home.

It is unusual for me to have spent such a long time away from my family. Even though I don't live with Mum and Dad anymore, I still see them regularly throughout an average week. A pang of longing jolts through me and I pull out my phone and call my parents.

"Hello, Ali-Cat," Dad says, answering the call.

"Hi, Daddy. How are you?" I may be twenty years old, but I will always be Daddy's little girl.

"Your mum is putting on a do for the street next weekend—so it is all hands on deck preparing for that."

I chuckle fondly. My mum has been known to go overboard when hosting—well, anything. For my thirteenth birthday, she made three times the amount of food needed for the size of the guestlist. And don't even get her started on her elaborate themes and décors.

"I miss you both," I sigh into the phone.

"We miss you too, Sweetie. Now tell me all about this tour! Are you being treated like royalty? I can't tell from your daily photos."

"It's pretty intense, Dad, but it's so amazing. I still cannot believe I am here."

"Just you wait. Soon it will be you headlining the tour. Everyone will know who Afterglow is and be buying tickets to see you, baby girl!"

I have always loved how supportive my dad is. Not that Mum isn't—she has always been a bit more *practical*.

"I know, Daddy," I reply with a laugh. "It's already starting to happen. The people are singing our songs along with us, and our merch stand is heavily depleted by the end of the night."

"And how are you getting along with the other band? I know they have been in the game a bit longer than you. Are they all being nice?" Dad asks, concern in his voice.

"They——" A knock at the door cuts me off.

"Ali," Mitch calls through the door. "It's time."

Crap.

"Sorry, Daddy. I got to go. I have a team meeting I need to get to."

"Ok, Sweetie. I love you."

"I love you too, Dad. Tell Mum I love her too."

"I will, now off you go—and keep those photos coming!"

Dad hangs up and, shaking off my homesickness, I leave my room and follow the noise to an open door down the hallway.

I peek inside to see both bands, Mitch, and Cecilia gathered, and it looks like I am the last one to arrive. Great.

"Ali, take a seat please," Mitch says as I enter the room. Not wanting to hold the meeting up longer than I already have, I quickly sink into the first available seat I see, which is on the couch next to Jax. Joel is in the armchair next to me.

"So, we wanted to give you all an update on the tour," Cecilia begins from her seat next to Mitch. It's always easy to tell when she is in "work mode," mainly because when she isn't working, you can find her attached to Maverick—sitting on his lap, cuddled in next to him, sharing a passionate kiss as if no one can see them. I long for a connection like they have.

"The sales have gone through the roof, tickets in the US are starting to sell out, and streamings have never been higher— for both bands," Cecilia says. "Fly By, it looks like the new album is a great hit, and 'Runaway' is quickly trending to be one of your most popular songs ever."

"Figures," Joel mutters under his breath. I don't know if anyone else heard his comment. If they do, they don't acknowledge it.

"And Afterglow," Cecilia continues, "Reckless Tunez is very pleased with how the audience is responding to you. We knew that being the opening act for Fly By would expand your listener audience—but we weren't expecting it to impact your sales so quickly."

"So, we have had an idea," Mitch adds. "We were thinking how great it would be if we released a collaboration between both of the bands."

"Ok. What does that mean exactly?" I ask.

"We would like you to write a song with one of the Fly By boys," Cecilia explains. "Specifically…Joel."

"What?" Joel exclaims, almost breaking out of his chair.

"You are both the lead singers, and we think it would be great publicity to announce that the two of you are writing a duet together," Mitch says.

I don't know what to think. I have no issue with collaborating with Fly By, but Joel clearly wants nothing to do with me. How am I meant to write a song with him? Especially with this unexplainable attraction I have to him. Why must I always like assholes?

"What do you want the song to be about?" I ask, trying to get as much information as I can. "What style are you thinking?"

"We were thinking something like a folk-rock. Pulling in elements of both the country-pop music and rock music that both bands are so good at respectively. We are hoping you can finish it in the next few weeks so we can use the popularity of the tour to promote and really capitalise on it. And given the current market trends—we want it to be a love song," Cecilia answers.

"NO!" Joel roars, getting to his feet at last. "No!"

Cecilia flinches slightly at his outburst, and Maverick stands, getting into his brother's face. My gut sinks through the floor. Now everyone will know how much he hates me.

"What the fuck is your problem, Joel?" Maverick demands.

"I am not doing it!" Joel protests.

"I can do it," Charlie offers, throwing me a disdainful look. What the fuck is the problem these brothers have with me?

"We don't want *you* to do it, Charlie. We want Joel to do it." Mitch says.

I sit there in my seat watching as Joel continues to protest adamantly that he won't do it. Clearly getting nowhere with his argument, Joel turns, narrowing those intense hazel eyes on me.

"Give me one good reason why you won't do it," Ethan says.

"What?" Joel whips around to face his youngest brother.

"Tell us all right now what this major issue you have is. You are being a fucking DIVA."

Tom and Maverick nod in agreement while Charlie throws Joel a look of sympathy.

"You think I am a DIVA?" Joel whines—literally, there is no other way to explain it.

"Yes. You have had a stick up your ass since Mitch told us Afterglow would be opening for us. We have endured your shitty attitude enough," Tom says.

"Fuckin' whatever!" Joel's shoulders sag, the fight going out of him. "You know, whenever you have shit going on, I am always there for you guys. When Maverick was having his shit go down, we were all there for him. But the moment that I have woman—" Joel cuts himself off. "Fuck!" he exclaims again, brushing past all his brothers and storming out of the room.

I watch him, my eyes following him with concern and confusion. What was he about to say? The door slams behind him and I turn back to see all his brothers' eyes focused on me.

What the hell did I do now?

8

Eight - Joel

THEY SAY KARMA IS A BITCH, but what the fuck did I do to
deserve this hell on earth? After the shit show that was the
"team meeting" yesterday, I was given no choice. I am
required to write a song with Alintia. A fucking love song
nonetheless—and in their hopes for getting this song
completed while we are on tour, I am now sharing a suite with
Ali until the song is written. A two-bedroom suite, thankfully. I
couldn't really ignore her before, but now we will be living on
top of each other until this song is done.

I walk out into the suite's living room and find Alintia sitting
cross-legged on the couch, expectantly waiting for me. She is
in a pair of grey yoga pants and a blue camisole. Her face is
free of all makeup and her hair is unrestrained again, showing
me those beautiful curls. My eyes linger on the curve of her
neck, which would look so perfect gripped in my hand.

Mentally shaking myself out of it, I cross over and plant
myself in the armchair across from her. I don't think I have
the willpower to sit next to her and not do something stupid—
not after the last time I was alone with her.

"So, where do you want to start?" Ali asks.

I only grunt in response, pulling out my phone and starting to scroll through anything to avoid looking at her. I am sure those piercing blue eyes will be able to see straight through me. She hasn't mentioned the kiss since it happened a week ago. More evidence that she doesn't want anything to do with me, I suppose. I don't know why she hasn't told anyone about it either. I basically attacked her. Surely if she reported that back to Mitch, he wouldn't have encouraged us to spend time alone together—trapped in this suite.

"You have to help me here, Joel. As much as I would like to take this off your hands and write the song for both of us— you have to have an input. You know they will be able to tell if you haven't added anything."

I grunt again. She isn't wrong, but I have nothing to say that can add to that conversation.

"I think we should brainstorm ideas first. If you don't want to actually write the song together, we can at least be on the same page and write separately before swapping or something."

"Mmhmm. It's a love song, what more is there to think about?"

"Oh wow, he speaks!" Ali says exasperatedly. "Is it a happy love song? Is it about a failed relationship, a tale as old as time, a plot twist? Are we singing first person, as if it were us in love? Are we singing third person, witnessing love happen in a different way? Is it a sexual love? Or a familiar or family love? There are options, Joel!"

"Shit, ok!" I say, dropping my phone in my lap and looking at her. "I didn't realise you wanted this to be so fuckin' detailed."

"Ugh! Just tell me what you want!" Ali yells.

You. I barely stop myself from uttering that damning word.

"You have clearly thought about this," I say, my voice surprisingly steady. "What are your thoughts?"

"Well, I don't know about you, but I have never really been in love," she says, her voice returning to her usual calmness—I assume it's because I am actually participating now. "So, I don't see how writing from my perspective would be good, depending on the theme we choose. Maybe we should pick that first?"

"I don't see how this is going to work if we have both never been in love," I grumble.

I need a break from all this fucking drama.

"I gotta go." I say, getting up and hightailing it back to my room.

"Wait, you should at least give me your number so we can text about this!" she calls from her spot on the couch.

"Not gonna happen, sweetheart!" I yell.

Within seconds, I have a pair of board shorts in my hand and am heading back out the door and out of the suite. I catch one final look of her before the door swings shut—and I swear I see a slither of tears gathering in her eyes.

Alintia

Two days have passed since we started sharing a suite, and Joel has been careful to never be alone with me. The first night, I tried waiting up for him to come back, only to wake up on the couch with a blanket thrown over me and his bedroom door locked. Last night I slipped out of the suite for five minutes to speak with Steph, Chris, and Jax, and when I came back, he had snuck into his room and locked me out again. He manages to sneak out each morning before I even get out of bed—sequestering himself in one of his brother's rooms, probably.

I have been playing around with the song—or attempting to, at least. How am I supposed to write a song from two perspectives about something I have never experienced? Since we were assigned this task, I have spent hours listening to other love songs, trying to get any ideas or motivation—but nothing is coming.

It would be easier if I had a direction, like I had spoken to Joel about—maybe I should just pick one and tell him "this is the theme of the song." But he is a rock legend, he is worth millions more than me, and he is clearly used to getting his own way. I can only imagine the hissy fit that he would throw if I wrote something that didn't reflect on him well. It doesn't help that Mitch and Cecilia are breathing down my neck with high expectations.

Thankfully, we have a sound check this morning for our concert tonight and that will get my mind off the asshole—at least for a little while. Never one to be late, I rise early, wash, dress, and make my way out of my bedroom and down to the bands' meeting rooms on this floor to wait for everyone else. I learnt early on that I cannot go ahead to the venue because it causes issues with security and travel arrangements. So, I sit here and wait for the rest of Afterglow to arrive and be ready to go. It was better when I was sharing a room with Steph since I could wake her up and ensure that she was up and ready to go on time—plus it gave me someone to talk to. Not just sit here alone like a loner.

I head over to the small kitchenette in the meeting room, taking the time to make myself a cup of coffee. It's no white chocolate mocha from Starbucks, but at least they have the good instant coffee, and not that crap you need to add a thousand sugars to just to get it down.

As I finish making my coffee, Chris swaggers into the room. I give him a wave which he acknowledges with a small nod before collapsing in the nearest chair and resting his head in his hands. Chris is adamantly not a morning person, so it is surprising that he is here first. Not that it is alarmingly early right now; it's only 10 am.

"Do you want a coffee?" I ask softly, to not alarm him.

"Nah," Chris grunts.

And that is it for that conversation.

I return to my earlier seat, conveniently located to see both the door and out the window. This tour really is going quickly. It's almost been three weeks—which only gives us three more to wrap up the tour in Australia and finish this song.

This song that is the bane of my life right now.

I pull out my phone and start scrolling through TikTok—I'm crazy addicted. I haven't posted any videos yet, but I know that soon I will probably have to keep up with social trends. At the moment, I am happy to just look through the app and seeing everyone else's creativity thriving.

Elation sweeps through me when I swipe to a video of two teenage boys dancing together to one of Afterglow's songs. They spin and twirl each other as text scrolls across the screen:

"This is my best friend. We tell each other everything, except one thing. I am hopelessly in love with him."

The taller boy on screen then pulls his friend into his arms, and as the chorus drops, kisses him full on his lips. The friend's arms reach up to the tall boy's shoulders as the taller boy pulls back. Their eyes meet for a moment before collapsing into each other's arms, laughing as the video ends.

I click on the sound and find myself lost in the joy of seeing our song be used for something so beautiful and meaningful to the people of this app. There are hundreds of videos that follow the same trend, kissing their crush for the first time, or even using the song in the background while they come out to their parents.

While I am lost in the TikTok world, Steph, Jax, and Cecilia have arrived—and now we are all ready to go to the arena for sound check. Ready to get this done, I put my phone away and follow the band down to the SUVs that will transport us to the venue—a new determination blossoming in my chest, all thanks to a TikTok trend.

We have done a few sound checks now, so it is pretty routine. Mostly, we just need to adjust the stage layout depending on any major size differences and ensure that the venue won't distort the sound or have any feedback—the sound technicians are good at their job and essentially leave us to just jam out and practice our songs while they sort that all out.

Sometimes it's overwhelming just thinking about how far we have come in this short time. A year ago, I didn't have a band, a future in the industry, or a fan base. Look at us now, preforming to arenas and venues with over ten thousand ticket holders, on tour with a band as famous as Fly By. It is everything I ever wished it could be—except that I am stuck with an asshole like Joel.

"How is the song coming along?" Cecilia asks once we wrap up sound check.

"It's harder than writing a song alone," I answer, giving her the truth without telling her exactly how bad it is.

"I'm sure you both will be able to handle it; Joel is experienced writing in collaboration with his brothers."

"But he doesn't know me like he knows them." Like that could even be the issue.

"So get to know him, then. That's part of the reason we have you sharing a suite. Close quarters and all that stuff. And perhaps you can even help J get over that girl."

"What girl?"

"You know the girl? The one everyone is talking about. The inspiration for Runaway. He wrote that song for the new album about ten months ago after meeting some girl. He is still hung up on her, but no one can get any information out of him—well, maybe Charlie."

I force myself to not roll my eyes. He must be so hung up on her when he flirts and kisses and beds groupies at every other after-party.

That is not your business—stop thinking about the hot, emotionally unavailable rock star.

I scoff mentally at myself. Like that could ever happen.

On my walk back to the Afterglow dressing room, I see the boys of Fly By and I know that I have to speak with Joel—

right this second before I lose my nerve. I square my shoulders as I stop in front of the brothers. They are all chatting amongst themselves, and I clear my throat to get his attention.

"Joel, can I speak to you please?" I ask as politely as I can manage, given my anger and frustration towards him.

"Can't now. Sorry," he replies without even looking at me.

"I really need to speak with you," I push. I really don't want to have this conversation in front of his brothers, but he isn't giving me much choice.

"We are about to go and do our sound check now that you lot are finally done, so no."

My shoulders sag. This really is hopeless.

"'Course he can speak with you. J, go with Ali," Maverick says, giving his brother a look that clearly challenges Joel to fight him on this.

"Not now," Joel rebuffs. "I'll talk to you back at the hotel," Joel says, dismissing me and turning on his heel towards the stage.

"That went about as expected," I mutter to myself.

"You just got to give him some time," Ethan interjects.

"Is this because of the 'Runaway' girl?" I ask.

"What do you know about that?" Charlie demands, glaring at me. Clearly, he has decided to make up for when his twin isn't around to torment me.

"Just what Cecilia told me? That he is hung up on a girl he wrote that song about."

"Seriously, Maverick?" Charlie turns his anger to his brother.

"What?" Maverick asks, confusion twisting his features.

"Why would you tell Cecilia about that?"

"I know you are not questioning the information I can share with my girlfriend. My girl is more trustworthy than all of the groupies you all sleep with. And—not that I have to justify myself to you—I didn't tell her. She picked up on that herself. Fuck, Charlie, we all have."

"It's not his fault!" Charlie yells, voice carrying down the empty hallway. I am all but forgotten now, just standing here watching the drama unfold between the brothers.

"Maybe you should calm down," Tom says, stepping in between Maverick and Charlie, roles I am sure they have all played before. "It's not like he can track her down. Joel tried for the first month, remember? He went to that coffee shop every day and even spoke with the barista about her. Why did he stop looking?"

"Because he found her," Charlie seethes.

"What?" Maverick, Ethan, and Tom say at the same time.

"He found her. That's why he stopped looking," Charlie continues, his voice dejected now.

"Did he talk to her?" Ethan asks.

"Yeah, but it didn't go well."

"What happened?" Maverick asks.

"I can't say," Charlie says, his eyes flicking to me.

"Do you mean…" Tom trails off.

I feel my cheeks heat as all eyes fall to me.

"Well, that clears a lot of things up," Ethan says.

"I still don't understand…" I mutter.

"Maybe this duet was a bad idea," Maverick says, hanging his head.

"FLY BY. SOUND CHECK NOW," Mitch's voice echoes down the corridor.

Without any words, the boys all head towards the stage, leaving me more confused than ever.

Nine - Joel

I HAVE MANAGED to avoid her for two days. I wish I could have squeezed out more time—for the sake of my sanity—but it looks like that is over now. As I walk down the corridor, their voices fading away, I hear my brothers patching the story together.

Fucking Charlie. Couldn't keep his mouth shut and leave well enough alone.

Now Maverick knows that I am a lovesick fool hung up on a woman who doesn't want me, which means Cecilia will know. So probably all of Reckless will know, too. Gossip is quick to spread while on tour. Which only means I will have to confront her. Fucking great. And to make matters worse—other than the fact that I am now essentially living with her—now I will have to avoid my brothers, too.

I shouldn't have told Charlie. I sure as fuck shouldn't have agreed to do the duet—not that I really had a choice, but I could have fought it more. I should have protested them even coming on tour—I have been proved time and time again that Alintia is the only weakness that I have in this world.

The moment my brothers step on the stage to do sound check, they all converge on me. Pitying looks in their eyes, apologies filling the air. I didn't want this. I scowl at Charlie, ignoring the others' sentiments, before going to my mic stand ready to get this sound check and stage rehearsal over and done with.

Avoidance is my game. I have avoided Ali for months now—although not always effectively. And now I am going to avoid this conversation with my brothers like the plague. The second we are done on stage, I escape out the side door and into the ally outside while my brothers are too busy with their instruments to notice me.

"Mr. Watson, can I help you?" a security guard whose name I don't know asks me from his position next to the exit.

"Uh, yeah. Can you organise for someone to take me back to the hotel, please?" This wasn't the escape I had in mind, but at least if I go with security, I won't be in shit for more than one thing today.

"Of course, sir," he replies, and starts talking into his radio. A few silent minutes later, one of our SUVs pulls up to the end of the alleyway.

"Thanks, mate," I say to the guard in farewell, hopping into the SUV without looking inside—too eager to get out of here.

Closing my eyes, I sag back into my seat, so ready for all this crap to be over. I have no problem being the centre of attention as a front man, but not when the attention is like this. I close my eyes, feeling a nap coming on. My early mornings getting up to avoid Alintia are catching up with me.

"Joel?" she says softly. Great, now I'm dreaming about her.

"What?" I snap.

"Are you okay?" Her soft melodic voice washes over me. I could stay here like this forever.

"Not really," I reply honestly, because this is my mind after all.

"Can I help?"

"You could give me a blow job. I have been fantasising about your sweet lips on my cock for months." I really shouldn't be indulging in this fantasy if I don't want to be hard every time I see her.

"Maybe when we get back to the hotel. I don't think we need an audience for that." She chuckles, the sound so beautiful I squeeze my eyes tighter, straining to hear as much as I can. But that laugh is too realistic—even for my crazy brain.

My eyes flash open to find Alintia sitting next to me. She is in the car with me.

"FUCK!" I jolt back. "What are you doing here?"

"I have been here since before you got in? I was already on my way back to the hotel when the driver said we had to pick you up too."

"Didn't you think to alert me to your presence?"

"Have we not just been talking? I was!"

Fuck, she's right.

"Just forget what I said…" I grumble, shifting to face away from her.

I feel her breath on my ear as she leans in, feel her breast brush against the back of my bicep.

"You mean you don't want me to suck your cock?" she purrs into my ear. So low the driver won't hear. So perfectly that my cock starts to harden in my jeans, making a very obvious bulge. "Do you want me to take care of that for you, Joel?" she continues in her sultry voice.

Before I can answer, the SUV stops, and we are back at the hotel. Ali gets out her side of the car, and I take a minute to rearrange my cock so it is not as obvious as we walk through the lobby.

Think unsexy thoughts! I desperately think of my brothers, and that does the trick. Boner is gone.

With a sigh, I get out of the SUV and head straight through the lobby and into the elevator. I must have taken too long or something because the lobby and elevator were blissfully empty of Ali. Now I just need to get into my room before she gets back.

I unlock the suite door and find out I was wrong… I was so very, very wrong. Greeting me is the sight of my—*not mine*—Ali. Kneeling on the couch in her jeans, her shirt discarded somewhere. Her beautiful brown torso is on full display—hidden only by a blue lacy bra.

"Took you long enough," Ali says, curling her finger, calling me forward. I have no power here. I am not able to resist her any longer. My feet carry me towards her.

Ali's hand reaches out and rests against my stomach as I stand in front of her. My body tenses under her touch, eager and desperate for her to never stop touching me. On her knees on the couch, she comes up to my chest, giving me a strange feeling of dominance—even though she is the one in control here. Her soft hands reach under my shirt and trace the lines of my abs, causing a shiver to race up my spine.

"What are you doing?" I ask.

"What you asked me to."

"Y-you don't have to," I stutter as my body breaks out in goosebumps.

"I want to, Joel."

Getting a handle on myself, I step back and out of her reach.

"Is this out of pity? Just because my brothers found out about us doesn't mean you need to do this!"

"I don't know what you are talking about," she whispers, hurt and confusion lacing her voice.

"I knew nothing had changed! I am such a fucking idiot!" I turn and quickly walk away.

"Joel—" Ali calls, but it's too late. My bedroom door slams, cutting her off.

What a fucking idiot. I could have just kept my mouth shut and her lips would be on my cock right now. Why does this woman have me so twisted up?

Without thinking too hard on it, I have my phone out and I am calling Mitch.

"Hey, Mitch. We need to talk," I say, my voice grave.

"Are you breaking up with me?" he replies, jokingly. "I thought I meant something to you!"

"Fuck. Be serious for a minute."

"Alright mate, what's up?"

"I need out of this duet and suite deal. I cannot fucking do it."

"Why? Is she not cooperating?" Mitch's voice suddenly stern.

"No, it's not that," I sigh.

"Then what is it?"

"I-I can't say. But I need to get out of this!"

"Joel, I probably shouldn't tell you this, but I am going to be real with you here. This duet wasn't my idea. It came from Reckless. They don't ask, they demand. If this song is something that cannot be done, they will need to know why. And more likely than not, they will blame Ali and Afterglow for its failure."

"You mean Afterglow would be kicked off this tour?" No matter how much I struggle being around her, I don't really want that—do I?

"I mean Reckless would drop them as a client entirely. They are only on a one-album contract. They won't see any contract negotiations until they prove to be successful and in high demand. I really struggled with getting them to be on a tour at all, let alone a tour for a band as prestigious as Fly By. This duet is a part of that.

"You and your brothers have it easy," he went on. "You have been established for a long time now, and usually you can ask for whatever you want, and Reckless will give me anything to make it happen. But I want you to be aware. If you don't do this duet, Afterglow's careers are basically over. If they get dropped from a contact, other labels aren't going to want them, no matter how good they are as musicians."

"That's not what I want," I mutter into the phone.

"So you have to do the duet."

"Fine," I grumble, hanging up on Mitch without bothering with a goodbye.

Taking a deep breath, I walk back into the lounge room. Ali is still sitting there, her eyes tinged red, her face flushed, while she is pulling her shirt back on.

Shit.

If I am going to do this duet, I am going to need a lot of fucking alcohol.

Ten - Alintia

ANOTHER ASSHOLE, another rejection. What is new there? Nothing. And what's worse is I should have expected it. The last few weeks have proven to me what type of person Joel is towards me. How can I expect a few sweet moments and a kiss to overpower the anger and hate that he has towards me?

I can't. Anger surges through me, and as it normally happens when I am angry, tears fill my eyes. I wish I was a normal person when it came to expressing my emotions. But I have always been an angry crier.

Pulling my shirt back on, I sit up as Joel opens his bedroom door, stepping out looking like a man about to be executed. What wonders this man does for my ego.

"Alright. I'll do the stupid fucking song," he grumbles, sauntering his way over to the minibar.

"What the fuck makes you think I want to do it with you after all this shit?" I ask.

"Neither of us have a choice, sweetheart," he says, pulling out a mini bottle of jack—about the size of a shot—and drinking it straight. "I just got off the phone with Mitch. If I pull out, you are out of the tour and out of a contract. Unfortunately, we don't have the luxury of saying no to writing this fucking thing."

"W-What?" I knew he didn't want to do it, but I didn't know that I would be blamed for that.

"Yeah," he continues, opening up a small bottle of tequila and swallowing it down. "So, you and I are gonna get this stupid thing over and done with right the fuck now. I am not dragging this shit out any longer than I need to endure it."

I sit there frozen in shock, this asshole man—who is hot and cold with me—is going to do this so I don't lose my contract?

"Why?" I whisper, my throat squeezing shut.

"Who the fuck knows? But I know I need to be drunk for this… Did you want one?"

I consider saying no. But honestly, one drink might help me break down what the fuck is going on right now.

"Ok. Just one, though." He hands me a mini bottle of vodka, and I knock it back without hesitation. "Let's get started before you are too wasted."

"Have you thought of a theme yet?" he asks, flopping down on the couch next to me.

"I was mainly waiting for you, to be honest. I didn't want to start to only have you rip it up."

"Wow. You must think me an entitled ass," he mutters, and I almost miss it.

"I do," I reply honestly, the words slipping out without my permission. A flicker of pain shows in his hazel eyes and I instantly want to take it back.

"Right, well, we know it has to be about love. And no matter how many options you spouted off the other day, we know what they want is a first-person love story. So we will have to stick with that."

"But should it be happy? Or sad?"

"The only kind of love I have experienced like that has been sad for me, so maybe that is the only way to go?"

One drink turns into two drinks, and as the night goes on, I lose track of how much we drink. We had all but left the song where it was when we both realised how hopeless we are at writing this song together…which is when we started drinking more. The conversation fell into weird conspiracy theories that we have both heard about and lapses of silence while we both just sat next to each other. It was nice to not be alone in this moment.

"We should be writing the song," I slur somewhat.

"Song is a stupid idea," Joel hiccups from his seat on the couch next to me. He moved here when we started passing a bottle of wine between us. Who can be bothered with glasses? I would probably break one right now, anyway. "We can't write a love song. Maybe we should write a sex song. At least we both know about that—right?" His eyes meet mine, like he is genuinely interested in my answer.

"If you are asking if I am a virgin, the answer is no. But I can't say I have ever had any amazing, mind-blowing sex."

"You're missing out. I am great at sex. Been too long for me though. I am just with ol' righty now," he admits with a sigh.

"Dude." I giggle. "How is that something you need to tell me?" I fall against him, my laughter shaking my whole body. "Besides," I murmur, while I definitely don't nuzzle into his shoulder, "I have seen you with those girls at the after parties —do you mean to tell me that you haven't fucked them?" Heat flares in my cheeks.

"Haven't been able to. My cock is only interested in one person at the moment." There is something in his tone that urges me to look at him. Drawing my head back from his solid body, I meet his gaze. His warm hazel eyes are filled with a look I have never had directed my way before—desire and urgency, like if he doesn't have me this second, he will die.

"M-me?" I stammer out, lust coiling in my gut. Ever since I laid eyes on Joel, I have craved his touch, his taste. I was so close with the offered blow job earlier before he shut that down. Is this finally my chance? Really, I shouldn't even consider it after all the mindfucks he has given me.

"Yeah. You, Alintia." The way he purrs my name has shivers racing up my spine. Unable to tear my eyes away from his, I see the moment he makes the decision—he isn't going to pull back this time. I can tell myself I won't do this as much as I want, but I'd be lying.

Unable to hold back any longer, I lean into him, so close our chests press together as our lips meet in a soft brush that is barely a kiss. As if my kiss unlocked something within Joel, he deepens the kiss, our tongues rolling together as his hands move down my back—urging me closer and closer. Unable to get much closer at this awkward angle, I take some initiative—

without breaking the kiss, I twist my body around and straddle his lap as Joel groans into my mouth.

Joel hands linger on my hips as he pulls back from our kiss, enough to talk but so our noses are still touching.

"Can I?" he moans.

"Can you what?" I ask, acting demure.

"What can I do? What can I touch?" His breath hot against my mouth.

I know there is no way I will regret any of this tomorrow—I have craved this for too long, wanted him for too long. No matter how much alcohol is in either of our systems right now, I know I will never forget this night.

"You can touch everything. You can do anything," I whisper against his mouth.

Joel reclaims my mouth in a bruising kiss as his hands move around to grip my ass, pulling me even closer, sitting me directly on top of his hard cock. The feel of hardness pressing against me only turns me on more. Our clothes are the only barrier between us and I want—I need—them gone.

As if we had the same thought, his hands move to the hem of my shirt as I curl my fingers into his. We break the kiss only long enough to pull each other's shirts off before crashing back together. His hot skin pressing against mine, curly chest hair tickling across my breasts. Joel quickly unhooks my bra with one hand, while the other is on my ass, squeezing in between my skin and my jeans.

"Wait," I huff, pulling back from the kiss so I can unbutton my jeans. Joel's mouth continues down my neck, lingering at my collarbone before trailing down to my boobs. "That better?" I ask as his hand slides deeper into my pants—now that my jeans aren't as tight.

"Mmm," he groans before sucking my nipple into this mouth. I arch into his mouth, simultaneously pushing my ass further into his hand and grinding my throbbing pussy against his cock.

"Please," I moan, "please Joel—I. I need…"

"What do you need, baby?" Joel asks, pulling back and meeting my eyes.

"Everything."

A wicked grin spreads across his face, and with both hands on my ass, Joel stands up, hoisting me up with him. A squeal escapes me as I wrap my arms and legs around him.

"What are you doing?" I ask, panic in my voice.

"Taking you somewhere you can be properly ravished," he says, heat curling inside of me at his gravelly voice.

Joel shoulders open his bedroom door and drops me onto the bed. Before I can even catch my breath, he is yanking my jeans down, my panties going with them. Lying here naked on Joel's bed, I feel like all my deepest desires are going to come true.

"Look at you," Joel says, almost reverently.

I watch him standing over me—shirtless, hair ruffled from my hands, lips lightly swollen, desire pooling in those hazel eyes. There's only one problem.

His jeans.

They do nothing to conceal the shape of his hard dick, but they are still on and in the way.

Sitting up, I reach towards him.

"My turn," I purr, meeting his heated eyes as I unzip his jeans. Hooking my fingers in both his briefs and jeans, I pull them both down at once, leaving him blissfully naked—ready for my eyes to devour him. His cock bounces back against his lower stomach, and I break our eye contact to look down at his manhood. It is thick and long, pointing straight at me like it knows exactly where it wants to be. A bead of precum emerges from his slit as my eyes take Joel's length in.

I dart my tongue out, flicking across the swollen head and collecting his precum. A burst of saltiness explodes against my tastebuds. Instead of sucking him into my mouth, I tease him, placing soft kisses and licking across his stomach. I grip his hands, and as I lie back down, pull him down with me. His legs entwine with mine, hot skin pressed against hot skin. Our mouths meet in a soft brush, more breathing the same air than an actual kiss.

Joel deepens the kiss, pushing his tongue against mine with a moan. His hands are everywhere, on my breasts, my ass, tangled in my hair. I feel his presence everywhere as he lies with his body over mine. I have never given much thought to any kinks, but there is something about feeling all of Joel's weight pressing down on me that is only enhancing my emotions.

"Please," I gasp into Joel's ear as he kisses down my throat.

"What?" Joel asks in a deep growl, pulling back to look down at me.

"I—I need…"

"What do you need, Alintia?"

Oh God! The way he says my name has shivers racing down my spine.

"I need you to fu-fuck me," I pant.

Joel's hazel eyes swirl, hypnotising me with their depths, full of heat and desire.

"Say my name," he commands, shifting his body so he is lying between my legs, his cock rubbing against the top of my mound.

"Joel," I moan. "Please, Joel. I need your cock in me."

With my words, Joel pushes his cock into me, my pussy quickly gripping around him.

"Fuuuck!" Joel groans. One hand next to my head to keep him propped up, and the other cupping my breast. My nipple hard and sliding against his rough palm.

This is not lovemaking. This is hard and fast fucking. And I love it.

Joel thrusts into me again and again, driving all the way in until there is no more cock to give me. Grinding slightly when he bottoms out, simulating everything at once. I have always had to work for orgasms in sex, often needing to direct my lover, or take matters into my own hands—but not with Joel. It's like my body is the melody, and he is playing it within an inch of his life.

"I—I'm cu—" My brain switches off as pleasure I have never known courses through my veins—my orgasm slamming into me suddenly.

"Yes, cum on my cock, Ali," Joel pants against my mouth.

Pulling out of me, he deftly flips me onto all fours. Before I can catch my breath, Joel is entering me again, his hands both demanding and caressing.

"Fuck. Fuck." We are both panting and cursing as Joel's balls slam against my clit as he thoroughly fucks me. I have never been fucked this rough—but I might never be able to do slow and tender ever again. My nerves are all on edge, his thrusts working my pleasure higher and higher.

"I need you to cum again," Joel growls.

Again? I usually barely have one. "I can't."

"No such word. You can. You will." Joel fists my hair, pulling me up with it until we are both kneeling, his chest pressed against my back, his other hand gripping my breast. His thrusts pick up, demanding more pleasure from my body.

Tweaking my nipple as he bites my neck, Joel urges me to fall apart with his name upon my lips. Joel's thrusts stutter, as if he were holding out for me. He groans, kissing my neck as he pushes into me a final time.

"Shiiiiit." Joel groans as he pulls out of me. I can feel his cum following his path and realise that we didn't use a condom.

"I'm on birth control," I say. "We're ok."

A huge sigh releases from him. "I'm glad, but I have never been so reckless before. I always remember to wrap up. Fuck." Joel falls down onto the bed, and I only hesitate for a second before I lie down next to him.

"I am just going to lie here for a minute, then I will go back to my room," I murmur, blinking my heavy eyelids.

I think Joel says my name, but I can't be sure as the blackness of heavy sleep claims me.

Eleven - Alintia

TONIGHT'S CONCERT was more amazing than any of the others so far. Every time, more and more people sing along to our songs, but tonight there was dancing, there were phones in the sky recording, and I even noticed a few people in the front rows doing that TikTok dance with our song.

I have barely seen Joel at all today. Waking up alone in his bed was a slap in the face. I still had his cum in me and he was already back to avoiding me. I'm not sure what else I was expecting. I have had drunken one-night stands before, but I thought we had…something. He knew my body better than even I do. I'm not saying I was expecting love and flowers this morning, but I didn't realise that I meant so little.

I had gathered my clothes and spent the day soaking in the tub, topping it up with hot water when needed, until it was time for me to go meet the rest of Afterglow. Catching sight of the several mini bottles of alcohol on the coffee table was a stark reminder of how I succumbed to him last night, and I needed to distract myself with something—anything—before

I started writing a Taylor Swift level of breakup song and we weren't even together!

Standing against the far wall and zoning back into the after party, I feel overwhelming happiness—not even the events of the last twelve hours with Joel can dim this feeling. To think of how far we have come, and the potential we still have to go—I was always hopeful, but I never thought I would get there.

"So, how does it feel to have a song written about you?" Steph asks, leaning against the wall next to me.

"The duet isn't about me; it's just imagined emotions. We aren't actually in love with each other," I laugh softly. Who even knows if we will be able to finish it now?

"That's not what I heard," she replies with an impish grin.

"What do you mean?"

"I heard a little rumour is all."

"What was it?" I sigh in resignation. This kind of gossip—it is almost always exaggerated.

"Well, some of the sound crew overheard your little spat in the hallway after our sound check yesterday with Joel, and some pieces were put together."

"Get to the point faster," I demand. Clearly this is information she thinks I already know, or should know, if she thought to bring it up at all.

"Jeez, woman. I heard that you were the inspiration for 'Runaway'."

"That's ridiculous, of course I'm not." My mind flicks over everything I have heard about the elusive Runaway. Joel met her almost a year ago, in a café…in a Starbucks café…his brothers call him J sometimes…

Wait—am I?

I feel sick to my stomach, my happy high from moments earlier crashing down around me. It can't be true. He can't be Jay. I would recognise him. Jay didn't have a beard, and his hair was shorter, and I would remember his tattoos—right?

The room around me swims as I stand there panting. Concerned hazel eyes meet mine before the world goes black.

"Alintia?" a deep, urgent voice asks at my ear.

My eyelids are heavy, and I fight to try and open them.

"Ali, baby, are you alright?" he asks again. The voice of my pain, my joy, my torment. Joel.

"I don't understand what happened," a voice I recognise as Steph says. What are they both doing in my bedroom? "We were just talking, then she just fainted and passed out on the floor." Ok so apparently, I am not in bed, I am on the floor.

"Did she drink anything? Does she have any allergies? Fuck." Joel growls before shouting, "Where the fuck is the first aid guy?"

"They are coming, bro," another voice—Ethan?—says. "Do you want me to help you move her to another room? It will be quieter and more comfortable for her."

Joel doesn't respond, and I try to open my mouth to tell them I am fine. That I can hear them. But it's like my jaw is wired shut. I can't open it. My eyes still won't open. I feel arms circle around me, tight and possessive, as I am lifted off the floor and carried somewhere. Joel's lips press against my ear, with a light lingering kiss, and soft words spoken in my ear as I fade out again.

"Alintia, I love—"

Twelve - Joel

I CARRY Alintia until we are back in our suite. Thankfully, tonight we had the after-party back at the hotel, and not at the venue like normal. Steph follows me in helping me get Ali lying flat on her bed. We are lucky that Steph managed to catch her mid-faint so she didn't hit her head.

"What the fuck were you talking about?" I growl, turning to Steph.

"Just you and the song. That's it. I swear," she replies, panic in her voice.

Mitch rushes through the door with who I can only assume is the first aid person for the tour. I want to growl at him on sight. Why did it take so long to get here?

"She's fine," he proclaims a few minutes later. "All her stats are normal. Without her being conscious or a CT scan I can't be sure, but I suspect she only has a minor concussion."

"Then why is she still asleep?" I demand.

"She is coming to now. Fainting spells affect everyone differently, and she has probably been in and out for a while now," he confirms.

"J…?" she croaks.

"Ali!" I rush back to her side, sitting on the edge of the bed and grasping her hand softly.

"Why?"

"Why what?"

Her eyelids fly open, and I can finally see those bright blue eyes again.

"Why didn't you tell me?" she asks, her voice both angry and hurt.

"What do you mean?"

"   about that day in Starbucks? Why didn't you tell me that was you?"

I feel my eyes widen in surprise. "You didn't know?"

"Huh?" she asks, the anger leaving her face as it twists with confusion. "Of course I didn't know."

"I thought…I thought that you—" I break off, unable to finish the sentence.

"We'll get out of your hair for a bit, looks like you guys need to talk," Mitch says, reminding me that we weren't alone.

I look around the room, seeing Steph, all my brothers, Cecilia, and the first aid guy getting ushered out the door by Mitch. I can't even think about all the gossip that could stem from this —I'm too focused on getting to the bottom of this with Ali.

"Why did you push me away?" Ali asks, drawing my gaze back to her face. She is pale and still recovering from her faint.

"I thought I had to," I say, unable to be anything but honest with her. "I tried to find you after that date. When I realised that you were called by Reckless, I started going to the studio more often in the hopes of seeing you. Then that day when Mitch introduced us…you recognised me, knew who I was straight away, and started going on about Fly By and how excited you were to be with the same label. I figured out that if you knew who I was in that moment, that you had always known. That you noticed me at Starbucks and thought that I would be a good backup plan if your demos didn't work out. But you got the call and abandoned me. You didn't need that anymore, so that's why the date never went anywhere."

"Joel—"

"Then the tour started," I continue, cutting her off. "You confirmed that you knew who I was since the beginning. I thought that was you trying to tell me that you didn't want me, that you didn't feel for me the way I felt for you."

"But I didn't know."

"Please don't lie to me," I whisper, looking away from those intoxicating blue eyes. "You had to have known."

"No, I really didn't. I must admit, even though I remember our Starbucks date, and our connection, the memory of your image faded in my mind."

I flinch back from her. I don't want to hear this, but I know I need to if I am ever going to move on from this—with or without her.

"That day… The reason I left was because Rachel called me. I left you and went straight to the studio. You know how much I wanted to get my break in the industry. And I figured that I could get *your* number from Chloe… When I got through everything with Reckless and came back to earth, I realised you weren't even my blind date, and I couldn't find you. I spent so much time thinking about what you must have thought about me, the random woman who just forced you into a date. No matter what instant connection we had, I tried to not hold onto the hope of finding you. I figured the chances were too low, and I would never be that lucky."

I look at her, meeting her eyes again.

"Then I met you—" she went on, "Joel, I mean—and everything started on tour. I was drawn to you, and it pushed Jay to the back of my mind. I wanted you. You made me feel both wanted and hated, and I couldn't understand it. Couldn't understand why that was pulling me to you. Then every time we would take a step forward, you would push me away again."

"I thought I was protecting myself," I offer lamely. "I couldn't resist you either, but I thought if I kept my distance, you couldn't hurt me more."

"And last night?"

"Do you regret it?"

"No. Do you?"

I feel a weight leave my chest in relief. "I was more worried that you would."

"Is that why you left before I could wake up this morning, and have avoided me all day?"

I feel myself blush. "That was part of it," I reply, sheepish. "I was worried you would wake up hungover, regret what we had done, and push me away again. Or worse, that you were going to use me."

"Come here," Ali says, tapping the spot on the bed next to her.

Kicking off my boots, I pull off Alintia's shoes and stretch out on the bed, lying down next to her. Without thinking, I open my arm, and Ali cuddles into my side, resting her head on my shoulder.

"You would think for two people who are really good at writing songs and expressing our feelings, we would have better communication skills," she says, laughing softly.

We lie there cuddling in silence. Not needing to say anything more between us right now. There has been enough soul baring tonight.

Just as I start to drift into sleep, Ali's phone rings loudly through the room. She quickly pulls it from her jeans pocket, glances at the screen, then answers.

"Hey, Daddy," she says sleepily. The phone is so close to my ear that I can hear him through the speaker.

"Are you ok, Ali-Cat?"

"I'm fine, Dad. What's with the late call?"

"We just got a Google Alert, there's a photo of you—"

"You know how to do Google Alerts?" Ali asks in surprise. "Why do you have a Google Alert for me?"

"Because you are our daughter, and you are becoming more and more famous by the day. We want to keep on top of all the stories and reviews about you and Afterglow."

"Aw Daddy, that's sweet," she murmurs, her voice still full of sleep.

"Anyway, Ali, there is a photo of you in all of these articles. Story is that you passed out drunk at the after-party? There is a photo of you in that other band's singers' arms. I thought you knew where your limits are and knew to not to drink irresponsibly."

"I didn't, Daddy. I fainted completely sober."

"Fainted? Are you ok? What's wrong?"

"She fainted? Oh, sweetie!" a female voice came through the phone with her dad.

"Hey, Mum. Yeah, I fainted. I am ok now though. I had a bit of a shock is all," she says, glancing up to meet my eyes with a small smile. "A good shock. I forgot to breathe for a second or two. I am fine now. First aid checked me over."

"We're glad you are ok, baby. You scared us," her dad says.

"I really need to rest now, and probably tell my manager to squash the rumours before it gets too big."

"Ok, Ali-Cat. Update us tomorrow, ok!"

"Ok. Ok. I love you."

"We love you too."

Ali hangs up the call and plays around on her phone for a second before putting it back to her ear.

"Ali?"

"Hey, Mitch. So, my parents just called me. Someone at the after-party took a photo of me, and the tabloids are saying I drank until I passed out. Do you think we can release a statement that I just fainted due to something minor and assure everyone that I am fine now?"

"Already on top of it. I didn't want to call and disturb you with Joel, but I have it handled okay."

"Thanks Mitch," I say into the phone, confirming that I am still here with her.

Ali pulls the phone away from her ear, Mitch having ended the call.

"Time to sleep," she mutters.

"Do you want to change?" I ask.

"Too much effort," she grumbles, but twists uncomfortably.

"Here, let me."

I pull away from her, quickly undoing and removing her jeans, leaving her in her panties. Gently, I roll her over and undo her bra underneath her shirt. "Pull that off," I order softly. Ali complies, doing that amazing thing where a woman removes her bra without taking off her shirt.

"Better?" I ask.

"Mmmhmm." She grumbles, "Get back in here."

Chuckling softly, I strip down to my underwear and, turning off the light, fall back into bed with her.

My Alintia.

I cuddle up behind her, spooning her as she rests her head back on my shoulder.

"Goodnight, Jay."

"Goodnight, my runaway girl."

Waking up next to Ali again stirred something within my soul. Yesterday when I woke up next to her, I was afraid I would confess how much I am in love with her when she woke up. I tried to supress it, to move on and push her away.

But after spending a night in bed with her—inside her—I just wouldn't be able to turn her away again. I would accept any scrap that she gave me, to any detriment of my own feelings. So I left her, naked in bed, my cum drying on her legs, and spent my day burrowed down writing the duet. The sooner that song was done, the better. For Ali, for the record company. I needed to get it done—we had already dragged it out and that was all my fault.

This morning, I did the same. I was wide awake at six a.m., and no matter how much I wanted to lie in bed with her all day, trailing my fingers, tongue, and kisses all over her body, I knew I had to get this song done. Pulling myself away from her had to be one of the hardest things I have ever done.

In all my months of speculating, craving, and wanting her, I never even considered that she hadn't known about me. My mind had immediately jumped to the worst-case scenario, and I had believed it. What did that say for my self-esteem?

Now, however, I had to do what an artist does best. Broadcast all my emotions into a song for the world to hear. For as much as we had struggled the other night to write the song, speaking with Ali last night had confirmed a lot of things for me, and as if that was all I needed, my brain unlocked itself. A melody and words rushing through me. It was all I could do to sequester myself away to get it all down on paper.

Thirteen - Alintia

FOR THE SECOND morning in a row, I wake up alone in bed after spending the night with Joel. If this keeps happening, it could give a girl a complex. This man has been, for lack of a better phrase, pining over me for the last year. And every time he gets me to himself or in bed, he leaves me alone. But lying here now, with Joel's scent on my sheets, it really starts to sink in. He is my Starbucks Jay—I am his runaway muse.

Holy. Shit.

I can't hear Joel in the suite at all. I had thought he might want to stay in bed this morning. After our explosive sex two nights ago, and our conversation last night, I thought we might have changed our trajectory.

I pick up my phone from the bedside table, and I call Chloe. The phone almost switches over to voicemail as she answers.

"Ali? Why are you calling me so earrrrrly! I thought you were some rock star now that doesn't get up until noon."

"Huh?" I check the time and realise it is eight a.m. "It's not that early, bitch. And I need to talk to you."

That got her attention.

"Spill. What happened?" I can hear her shuffling around in her bed, sitting up and giving me her full attention.

"So, I may have slept with Joel."

"YES!" she squeals. "I knew it! How was it!?" Even though she is a lesbian, we have always been very open with each other about our sex lives. Just because we aren't interested in the same gender doesn't mean we aren't besties who share everything.

"Fucking amazing. He sure knows his way around a bed."

"Ugh, you lucky bitch. So, why the early call? Shouldn't you be stirring him for round two?"

"That's the thing. This was the night before last that we had sex—"

"AND I AM JUST HEARING ABOUT IT NOW!"

"SHHH. I am getting to that! I woke up yesterday alone. Like he had left without waking me—either sometime in the night or early morning, I'm not sure. Then he avoided me all day. THEN, last night, I found out…you remember that blind date that you set me up on months ago with the guy from your work?"

"How is that relevant? I wanna hear about Joel, the rock god in bed!"

"Trust me! Do you remember how he didn't show? And I spent the hour talking with someone else, thinking it was your coworker."

"Yes."

"That was Joel!"

"NO!"

"YES!"

"NO! What? Really?"

"Yep! One hundred percent," I laugh.

"Get the fuck out!" Chloe squeals.

"I'm not joking."

"Jeeze, that's just… Wow. What are the chances?"

"I know. Steph told me. Apparently, the whole crew had figured it out. You know the song 'Runaway' from their new album?"

"Yeah?"

"That's about me, and our Starbucks meeting."

"OH. M. GEEEEE. I have to listen to that again!"

"But."

"Oh no! Not a but… What happened?"

I huff a sigh. "I didn't have a great reaction when I found out. I fainted. He cared for me, and we spoke about it until we fell asleep together—sans sex this time—but again this morning I woke up alone."

"Huh?"

"That's pretty much my thoughts. I thought…well, I don't know what I thought. It's not like we are dating or anything, and he doesn't owe me anything. But I kinda figured that he would stay."

"Have you tried to talk to him yet?"

"No. I haven't even gotten out of bed. I don't know what I would even say."

"Well, do you at least know what you want?"

"What do you mean?"

"Do you know if you want to be friends-with-benefits, boyfriend/girlfriend, just friends?"

"Not really…" I trail off.

"Start there. Figure out what you want, then speak with him. Don't settle for what he offers if it isn't what you want."

"Ahh. So that's why I keep you around—that excellent advice." I chuckle.

"That and I am a hot piece of ass." This is why I love Chloe. She always knows exactly what to say.

"Love you, bitch!" I say.

"Love you too, bitch! Have a good day and give him hell!"

We hang up and I just lie there. Staring at the ceiling wondering what it is about Joel that I can't turn away from.

Grumbling, I tumble out of bed and make my way into the shower. Nothing is going to get done until I no longer stink of dried sweat from last night's show.

I stood in the hot shower until the water started to cool and my fingers were prunes, running my mind over all the possibilities that would come from Joel. Did I want to just spend the rest of tour fooling around with him? Yes, but I didn't want casual, I didn't want fuck-buddies. There was a connection between us that I couldn't begin to explain—but I wanted to explore. I wanted the chance to be with him. To discover what that connection is and what it could develop into.

Resolving myself to finding him so we can talk about this, I dress for the day and get ready to go and find him.

As I collect my phone to leave the room, it chimes with a new message.

Steph: Band Meeting in the Jax and Chris' room. Meet us in 5.

Clearly Joel will have to wait. Afterglow needs me, and no matter how new we are, I know that I need to prioritise the band if we want it to work.

Grabbing the key to the suite, I head down the hallway and knock on the boys' door. We are all on the same floor in this hotel too, with little taped signs on each door with the occupants' names. I suppose this was to help us with finding our rooms and help security keep us monitored. No one aside from our road crew and hotel staff—that had been vetted and cleared—are allowed on this floor.

Jax answers the door, stepping aside to let me in. Steph and Chris are already sitting across from each other at the small table that the room has.

"Is everything ok?" I ask no one in particular, sitting down next to Chris.

"I think so," Jax says as he sits across from me.

Chris shrugs, keeping quiet in his usual "not a morning person" fashion.

"It was actually Cecilia who called this meeting. She just asked me to get you all here ready for her to join us," Steph says.

"Oh, okay," I say as there is a knock at the door. Jax gets up to answer the door again, stepping aside to reveal Cecilia, Maverick, and Mitch.

If this is about Joel, I am not sure if I am ready for this conversation.

They make their way to the couch next to the table, sitting down in unison while smiling at us.

"I should have thought about how many of us there are," Mitch says. "Should have met in the meeting room, but didn't want it to be too formal a meeting."

"Oh well," Cecilia says. "We are here now, and we can get this meeting done here. Doesn't really matter as along as we all have a seat. We wanted to talk to you all about your contract."

"Is everything ok?" Jax asks.

"Oh, yes! Everything is fine. Great, actually. Your streaming has skyrocketed, and we have had some enquiries about radio interviews and TV show appearances," Cecilia replies.

"Really?" we say in unison.

"Yes," Cecilia says with a chuckle. "We will be starting to schedule these interviews around the tour schedule. Some of the radio sessions may be over the phone rather than in studio, but they will all be given a list of questions that they can and cannot ask. Once these are all booked, you will be notified by either myself or Mitch, and we will be with you daily for any schedule keeping, etc. Does anyone have any issues with this?"

"No." "Nope," we each reply.

I cannot believe this is really happening. I thought we were lucky enough to have the album and tour deal. This is just insane.

"Great. Now we have the duet with Alintia and Joel in the works, which will be a single. But we need to talk about your next album," Cecilia continues.

"Our next album?" Chris says.

"Yes, now your current contract is only for the one album, which you have already released, and the tour that we are on now. With the way sales are going, Reckless Tunez wants to sign you again now."

What she really means is we have proven ourselves to be money-makers and they want to have us commit to them before someone else "steals" us.

"Do they have a new contract prepared?" I ask.

"Yes," Cecilia says, and Maverick, who has just been sitting quietly, hands us each a copy.

"You understand that we will be getting a lawyer to look over these, right?" I have heard too many horror stories of bands locked into six or more album deals with no control over their own sound.

"Of course," Mitch says. "We are hoping to have this finalised as soon as possible, but it does depend on how Ali and Joel's duet goes. You should also be aware there is a clause here"—Mitch indicates to the fourth page in the contract—"that states that Reckless can separate your band and reconstruct it, as Afterglow is their creation, and that at any time they can cancel the contract with no repercussions, such as if you fail to meet the terms of your contract. There is not a clause for you to back out of the contract without financial or legal repercussions."

"Thanks, Mitch," I acknowledge. He is a decent bloke, having him and Cecilia as our contacts with Reckless has been great. They are genuine and caring, and only want to ensure the best for us. Not every manger, producer, or agent is like that. I honestly don't see us not re-signing with them, and I know that Mitch and Cecilia will protect us from any major drama

—but I will still get a lawyer to look over the contract and confirm that my band is on board before we go forward.

"Speaking of that duet," Maverick starts, speaking for the first time since he arrived, "how is that going, Ali?"

"Uhh, it's a work in progress," I admit. "I haven't really spoken with Joel in the last few days, but we were working on it a few nights ago." Not that we really got anywhere with it. "I should probably go do some work on it so we can meet our deadline," I say, standing from my seat. "Guys, we can catch up alone later and talk more about the contract, but give it a read over and make any notes about what you want to discuss."

"Sounds good," Jax says.

I make my goodbyes to everyone, leaving the room and making my way back to our suite. I wasn't lying. I really should get to work on the duet. Even if Joel is back to avoiding me, it needs to get done.

Sitting down on the couch, I collect my notebook from where it was left only two nights ago and fall into my feelings—but really, how well can you write a duet one-sided?

I spend the rest of the day in our suite, playing around with lyrics and melodies, not really getting anywhere productive while I think over the last few months. Doing as Chloe suggested, I take the time to really think about what I want out of our situation and possible future with Joel.

Waiting minutes turns into hours. I was expecting Joel to come back to the suite before our concert tonight, but he still hasn't returned, and now it's time for me to leave to get to the venue on time. As the day ticks by, my anger bubbles. I thought we were past this—this manipulation game he is playing. I am over it.

I leave and head to the venue in the SUV with the rest of Afterglow. This is the last concert at this venue before we are on the road to the next city tomorrow. Confronting Joel can wait until the end of the show. If he isn't going to prioritise me, why should I be the one to seek him out again? How is it that after all this time on tour and sharing a suite together, I still don't have his phone number? I mean, sure, I could have asked his brothers, or Mitch and Cecilia even, but I didn't want everyone knowing what was going on between us. It is bad enough that they all know about our failed first date—how badly must they have all thought of me, playing Joel and stringing him along? Either way, after tonight's concert I'll talk to Joel and get this shit sorted out once and for all.

Fourteen - Joel

I DIDN'T MEAN to spend the whole day in the studio, but sometimes I lose my head in the song-writing progress and what feels like five minutes is actually five hours. At least I finished it—or well, I finished my side of it. I have to show it to Alintia so she can write in her sections, but other than that it is done. I was honest in the way only a man in love can be. Every emotion poured into the duet, which really turned into more of a ballad as I wrote. There was space for any changes that Ali thought we needed, but overall, I am happy with how it turned out. The melody wasn't too fast or slow, sitting perfectly in the middle, and included elements similar to the 80's power ballads I grew up on.

I had hoped to get back to her this afternoon before the concert tonight, but that didn't happen. Now there are only thirty minutes until Afterglow are due on stage. Standing over the toilet in the bathroom, the door flies open, crashing against the wall behind it. Even though my back is to the door, I know who it is: The same person it was last time, so many weeks ago.

"Can I help you with something?" I say, using the same words as last time, keeping my back to her.

"You can start with telling me why the fuck you are avoiding me again," Ali yells, fuming.

This was not what I was expecting. Zipping up my pants, I turn around to face her.

"What do you mean?"

"You have avoided me all day. I waited in the room expecting you to come back. After last night, I thought things had changed. I—" She cuts herself off, taking a deep breath—if I didn't know any better, I'd say she was trying to stop herself from crying.

"I was in the studio," I say in a placating tone, walking to the sink and washing my hands. "I wasn't avoiding you. I have spent the last two days finishing my side of the duet." I turn around and face her, drying off and leaning against the bench. "Time just got away from me, you know how it is," I offer with a shrug.

"You—you were working on the duet?" she asks, like that was the last thing she expected.

"I mean, I was just so focused on getting it all finished. I didn't want you getting in any trouble from Reckless. I know they were expecting us to have finished it already by now."

"What?"

"Yeah, so I finished it. Well, I need you to add your side, and we can tweak it together, but I got the melody down and yeah. I was planning to come talk to you about it this afternoon, but I ran out of time, so I figured I'd talk to you after the show to not distract you."

"You're not ignoring me?"

"No babe, never!"

"Well, you did a shitty job of showing that!" I can tell she is still angry, but she has cooled down as we've spoken.

"Get over here," I demand, pulling her to me and wrapping her up in a hug. Her body fits perfectly against mine, her head tucking beneath mine. I place a kiss against her forehead. The rest of her anger seeps from her body as she relaxes into my embrace. I pull my head back, hooking my hand under her chin and tilting her head so our eyes meet. "I'm never going to ignore you again—I always sucked at it anyways."

"Can I hear the song?"

"I only have my side of it, but yeah."

Without any music, and only the acoustics of the bathroom, I start singing the song I wrote for her, for us. Sure, it's something the record label asked us to write, but they couldn't put these feelings into my heart, or the words into my mouth:

A devil in disguise, a demon manifest.

An excuse for me to fall in love.

You've used me and pulled me apart to

A shattered husk of a heart.

YOUR BODY IS a sin that I wish to commit.

I'm in love with a succubus deep in Hell's Pit.

I get down on my knees, oh baby please.

Take me, break me, vilify and ravage me!

PARADISE, ain't far from those devil eyes.

And I'm terrified

That I'm still in love with you

Oh you

Paradise, I can't find it in strangers' thighs.

I keep coming back to you,

Oh you

You…

"Wow," Ali says once I finish singing.

"What do you think?"

"You really feel all that, for me?" she asks, awe in her voice.

"Yeah, baby."

She grins up at me, and I can't help but kiss her. I press my lips against hers softly. Even her lips fit perfectly against mine, her bottom lip in between mine—I bite down, enough to pull it further into my mouth without breaking the skin.

Ali moans and runs her hands over my back, pushing her tongue into my mouth, licking against mine. Our kiss quickly turns hot, just a combination of teeth, tongues, and roaming hands. My left hand ends up tangled in Ali's hair, my right hand gripping her ass. She is already in her stage makeup and outfit for the night, and I pull back, breaking the kiss.

"What's wrong?" she asks, breathless and lips swollen.

"There's only, like"—I look at my phone—"twenty minutes until you need to be on stage. If I keep kissing you, I'm not going to stop until we both cum."

"Mmm," she purrs, giving me a seductive grin. "Better make it quick then." She turns around, leaning against the bathroom bench, sticking her gorgeous ass out for me. She is in a skirt tonight, and she pulls it up, showing me her bare ass, covered only in a lace white thong.

"Ali," I groan. I could sink to my knees and worship this ass for the rest of my life. My cock is so hard, it chafes against my jeans, even with my briefs on.

"Yes, Joel?" she asks sweetly.

"You aren't being fair," I complain.

"Who wants to be fair? You can't tease and torment me, turning me on only to stop now. Come on, big boy." She looks at me over her shoulder, the movement catching my eye, and I meet her gaze above that perfect ass. "Fuck me, Joel," she commands.

Without any more protests, I unzip my jeans and pull out my aching cock.

"Is this what you want, baby?" I growl.

"Yes," she whimpers.

"I don't have a condom," I grumble. How can I always be so unprepared around her?

"It's ok. I told you—I'm protected. Just get inside me."

"Are you sure?" I ask as I drag the tip of my cock through her folds.

"Yes."

"You have to be quiet." I meet her eyes in the mirror, wild and desperate with her desire. Teeth biting down on her bottom lip, she nods, and I start to press inside her.

I try to go slow, but once the tip of my cock is surrounded by her wet, tight pussy, I thrust completely inside of her, unable to control myself a second longer. Ali squeals as I grind my pelvis flush against her ass.

"This is going to be quick, baby."

"Mmhmm."

My hands gripping her ass cheeks, Ali makes a noise of complaint as I pull my hips back—leaving just the tip inside—before snapping forward, thrusting completely inside of her. All hope at being quiet dissipates as the sound of my thrust against her wet pussy bounces off the bathroom tiles. The wet and filthy noises surrounding us, spurring me on even more. Thrusting harder and faster, grinding inside of her, dragging the tip of my cock against her pussy walls, feeling her body shiver and clench around me.

"Oh fuck. Oh fuck. Oh fuck," Ali pants breathlessly.

"You like that, baby? How about this?"

I leave one hand on her ass cheek, gripping and massaging the skin there, and wrap the other around the front of her body, tapping my finger against the top of her slit and hitting her sensitive clit.

"I'm...so...close..."

I flick her clit again, feeling her pussy clench around me. I lean over her body, pressing a soft kiss to the exposed skin on her neck.

"Cum on my dick, Ali," I breathe into her ear.

"Joeeeeel!" she screams as she creams all over my cock.

Pulling all the way out of her, I grip her hips roughly. Turning her around, I pick her up and deposit her on the bathroom counter. Eagerly she spreads her legs for me again, wrapping them around my torso as I step between them. Our clothed chests flush together as I crowd against her. I capture her mouth in a kiss as I sink back into her.

Our kiss is as rough as our sex, claiming and taking as our tongues tangle together. Her left hand grips my wrist where my hands are on the bend of either side of her, while her right hand twists into my hair, fisting it and pulling it slightly.

I redouble my efforts, pounding into her again and again. The wetness of her pussy wraps around me, driving my own pleasure higher and higher. I thrust harder and harder into her, once, twice, feeling her walls quiver in another wave of pleasure.

"Joel!" she cries out and I follow her with my own climax—eyes locked, the pureness of her ecstasy all over her face.

"Has anyone seen Ali?" one of the stage crew calls through the hallway outside the bathroom. "Afterglow are due on stage in five minutes and she is nowhere to be found."

"Fuck," Ali chuckles. "I guess I have to go." She smiles up at me, her natural sweetness twining with the pleasure I gave her. Pride swells within me knowing I gave her that.

"Yeah, I guess so." I kiss the tip of her nose, pulling away from her and grabbing my hand towel to clean us both up. Ali hops off the bench and turns to the mirror, adjusting her clothes back to normal. With a fluff of her hair, and a reapplication of her lipstick, you wouldn't be able to tell what just happened. A private memory for just the two of us, lingering behind and warming me up inside. I wrap my arms around her waist, curling around her and meeting her eyes in the mirror again.

"Go rock their socks off," I whisper, kissing her cheek before letting her go.

"You too, Jay."

I follow her out of my bathroom and into the chaos that is backstage.

"Alright, alright. I'm here. Let's do this!" Ali says, assuring everyone that she isn't missing.

Alintia rushes off towards the stage wings, and I follow at a more leisurely pace, finding a spot in the wings just as she finishes sending a message on her phone and steps out onto stage.

"Goodnight, Adelaide!" Ali's voice rings through the arena, the crowd calling out in excited squeals and applause.

I stand there for their whole set, indulging in watching Alintia strut about the stage, singing her heart out to everyone here. She is a natural performer, and watching her is an honour as well as a beautiful sight.

Fifteen - Alintia

PERFORMING for crowds this size never gets old. Each and every concert is special and amazing to participate in. Joel is watching in the wings, and feeling his eyes on me only makes me sing and perform harder than ever before. Not to impress him, but to match him, to show him that I am his equal.

I can't believe that I was daring enough to demand he fuck me in the bathroom backstage before the concert. I have never been a prude, but I have never been so ballsy and reckless all at once. There was just something about him, about that moment that I just needed to have him—to be with him.

I had planned on confronting him after the show, but that went out the window when I walked past his dressing room and heard him warming up his voice. I couldn't guarantee that I would be able to get him alone later, so I decided to corner him then when I could and make the most of it. And boy, did I.

On top of all that, the song. Our song.

Of all the things I thought he would be doing, I never thought he would be spending his time finalising my ideas from the other night and forming it into a song. A song full of love and passion that could rival all others—at least in my opinion.

Wrapped in his arms, hearing him sing softly to me, confessing all his thoughts and feelings is a moment I will never forget. It felt like the moment in *Dirty Dancing* when Baby finally does "the lift" with Johnny at the end of summer show.

Stepping off the stage and into Joel's open arms is a new experience, but one I could get on board with real fast.

"That was a great show!" he says, kissing my temple while he hugs me. I am a sweaty, tired mess. After the show, and the *excitement* beforehand, I could really go crash and sleep for hours.

"Thanks."

"Are you staying for the main act?"

"Of course," and I mean it. No matter how tired I am, he deserves to have my support as much as I have his.

Placing a kiss against my lips, he sadly lets me go. He steps around me to join his brothers next to the stage, ready for their set.

"Seems like you two have worked out your issues," Steph says, stepping up to my side.

"Yeah, I think so." I smile at her, happy to stand here in the wings and watch Joel perform for his adoring fans.

I have watched them perform countless times on this tour now, but nothing could compare to the energy that radiates off the stage tonight.

"Now guys, before we sign off for the night, there is one final song that we want to sing for you," Joel calls out to the crowd. "But I need to have a guest come out and sing it with me." He looks over to me in the wings, and even with all the blinding bright lights in his face, I know he can see me. "Ali, baby, won't you come out here?"

I don't know what game he is playing, but not one to say no, I step out onto the stage, joining Joel at the microphone. The crowd cheers as I stand next to Joel. He can't possibly think this is the time to sing the unfinished duet, can he?

"Now, you all know this song," Joel says, addressing the audience again. My shoulders sag in relief. It's not *the* duet—but what is it? We haven't prepared for this. "Boys." He nods to his brothers.

"What song is this?" I whisper to him, avoiding speaking into the microphone.

Joel just grins at me without a response. "One, two, three, four."

The second the melody starts, I know the song—and I know why he has pulled me up on stage to sing with him.

Brown heels, curly hair, eyes so blue you'd think they're the ocean.

I found you in a cafe downtown, my heartbeat stopped, and the world lost its sound.

Fell in love at first sight, don't know who you are but that's alright.

Are you even a fan of people like me? Long hair, dark clothes and all inked from my head to my feet…

Will you….

RUNAWAY TONIGHT! Let's runaway tonight.

Runaway tonight! Let's runaway tonight.

I KNOW people might not like the way that you walk, the way that you dress,

but you're the best thing I've ever seen baby.

We'll be followed by paparazzi and cheap magazines, you don't gotta worry cause I'll show you the real me. So when they're following us we'll just…

RUNAWAY TONIGHT! Let's runaway tonight.

Runaway tonight! Let's runaway tonight.

And if they ever come knocking on our front door, I'll go give em what's for and make them …

Runaway tonight! Go on runaway tonight.

· · ·

WE'LL BE **Bonnie and Clyde, ride till we die. Make sweet love every night.**

Talk about life and the weight of it all. Drive with the top down or fly to Nepal.

As long as we got each other, one way or another. There ain't nothing in this life that's gonna bring us down. So let's just...

RUNAWAY TONIGHT! **Let's runaway tonight.**

Runaway tonight! Let's runaway tonight.

And I'll be ok, even though I watched you runaway from me, I'll be here waiting for you so we can...

Runaway tonight! Let's runaway tonight.

Runaway tonight! Let's runaway tonight.

I share the microphone with Joel, singing along with him, adding a lighter layer to his vocals, continuing after the song ends, and the music trails off.

And I'll be ok, to run back to you

We'll be Bonnie and Clyde, and I'll show you it will be alright,

As we runaway tonight.

The crowd's roars fall away as I lock eyes with Joel. It feels like there is no one else in the world as he leans into me, kissing me—claiming me—in front of everyone.

"Ladies and gentlemen, my Runaway girl," Joel announces, indicating me to the crowd. "Goodnight, Adelaide!" we chorus unintentionally, causing me to laugh as we make our way off stage. Joel's comforting arm wraps around my shoulders.

"So, how is the duet going?" Cecilia asks Joel and I, sitting in the SUV back to the hotel after the VIP Meet and Greet.

"Almost done," I reply. "Just a few things left to add, then we should have it ready for you."

"Would this sudden change have anything to do with the 'Runaway' performance and kiss on stage?"

"More so the other way around," Joel says, smiling at me.

Sixteen - Joel

IS this how she felt when I avoided her for days at a time? For the last three days I have barely had a moment with her alone. All her time off stage has been spent with her band, doing contract negotiations or doing interviews. And when we get back to the hotel, she passes out from exhaustion before we have the chance to talk.

I understand why she is so busy. I remember what it was like for us on our first tour, and how crazy it can still be at times—but I wish it didn't feel like I was being left out. Which doesn't even make sense. I am happy for her. Proud of where she is at and willing to support her to get to the next level, if that is what she wants. I just want to spend time with her too.

We haven't even had the chance to sit down and finish the duet—you would think the label would ease up on the schedule a little bit to allow us time to do that, but when I brought it up to Mitch, he just told me we should have already had it done, and to find a way to make it work out.

The crew seem to have accepted our sudden relationship—if I can even call it that yet—with ease. We haven't even had the chance to talk about what we are now. I mean sure, we have slept in the same bed every night, but when I wake up—she is already gone. I see her around the concerts, and we kiss and cuddle at the after-parties, but never alone—never with the time to tell her how much I love her. That I want her to be my girlfriend, not that it is a strong enough word for what I feel for her—what she is to me.

We need to start somewhere though. Chemistry and explosive sex don't always transfer over to relationships. We need to actually date, actually get to know each other when I am not being an asshole to her.

Today is a rest day. No concerts. No traveling to a new city. No media. No prior arrangements. Nothing.

Except I woke up alone. Again. Reinforcing for me how cruel I had been to Ali. After our night backstage in the bathroom, we exchanged phone numbers to prevent a blow up like that again. I scoop my phone up off the bedside table. It's nine in the morning, no messages or notifications. *Awesome.* I flick Alintia a text asking where she is at, and I get ready for the day. Maybe I can find her so we can actually spend some time together.

Showered and dressed, I still haven't received a reply from Ali. Without an idea on where she is, there is no point in trying to look for her. She could be anywhere, even out in the city shopping. Grumbling to myself, I leave our suite and head over to Charlie's room.

I don't bother knocking and just enter into his room. He had given me a key to his room for just this purpose. Charlie was in bed asleep, so I flopped down on the bed next to him, jostling the bed enough that he woke up.

"The fuck?" Charlie slurs.

"Oh, good. You're awake."

"Dickhead," he grumbles, rolling over to look at me. "What do you want?"

"Bored."

"Don't you have some sexy brunette sharing your bed? Shouldn't you be in that bed with her, and not here with me?"

"She's out."

"What did you do to fuck it up so quickly?"

"Thanks for the vote of confidence."

"Are you telling me you didn't fuck it up?"

"I dunno, man," I sigh. "We haven't really had the chance to talk and get everything really settled between us. The tour and publicity are always getting in the way."

"You're not still giving her an icy mix of passive aggression and just plain aggression, are you?"

"I know, I know. That whole thing was me overreacting, basically. I should have confronted her that first day," I say, wiping my hand over my face. "I could have prevented all this bullshit."

"And been with her months ago," Charlie interjects, *helpfully*.

"Right," I grumble. "Be thankful you don't have my stupid when it comes to the female population."

"I wouldn't be so sure about that."

"What happened?" I ask, instantly concerned for my brother.

"Just some bullshit with Gwen. She has stopped talking to me, says her boyfriend isn't comfortable with our friendship."

"That's bullshit! She's never let a guy get between you guys before."

"I know. I am looking forward to being home next week so I can talk to her about it in person. Something about this boyfriend is just giving me a bad feeling."

"Sure you don't just hate him cause he is with the woman you love?"

"Fuck off. I am just glad this part of the tour is almost over."

For a tour I was dreading to start, it sure has gone quickly and now I don't want it to end.

"A week to catch up with Mum and Dad, and then chill out before heading to America. Can't wait."

"At least Ali lives in the Gold Coast too, right? Maybe you will get to see her before they fly to America with us."

"Hopefully. Who knows? I might even convince her to come meet the folks." A picture flashes through my mind. Alintia talking with my Dad, having coffee with Mum. Goofing around with my brothers and I in the garage.

"You think she is ready for that?"

"Well, she can put up with you four—what's Mum and Dad compared to that!"

"True!" he laughs.

"So, back to Gwen. Maybe it's time to go on some dates," I say, tentatively.

"There hasn't been anyone since about nine months ago, honestly, and even that woman couldn't really hold my interest," Charlie says seriously. "I took her home with me mostly because I was drunk and she was persistent. I was glad she left before I woke up in the morning."

"That's surprising!" And it was. Most women who my brothers and I take home try to stick around as long as possible, hoping to get in on the band gossip or become a girlfriend. "Did she steal anything?"

"No," Charlie laughs, bringing him out of his sombre mood. "She didn't leave anything either. No name or phone number. Not that I really wanted to contact her, but it was a bit confusing to be honest. I haven't really thought about her since. The sex wasn't great, thanks to my being wasted and all, but as I said, I haven't been interested in anyone since."

"Maybe it's time to go after Gwen," I suggest lightly.

"I told you," Charlie says exasperatedly, "she has a boyfriend. She *always* has a boyfriend."

"So?"

"Just drop it, Joel," Charlie huffs, rolling over onto his back to stare up at the ceiling. "I gave up on that a long time ago."

"If you gave up, you wouldn't still be pining after her—just saying."

"Joel," Charlie protests.

"Just—" I pause, waiting for him to look at me. "Just learn from me, okay? I thought she knew. Thought she was playing her own little game with my heart. Turns out I was wrong. Have you ever flat out told Gwen how you feel?" Charlie glares at me. "I'll take that as a no. So do it. At least you get it off your chest and you know for sure."

"I'll think about it," he relents. "Now are you going to tell me why you are here?"

"I already told you. Alintia is out and I am bored."

"You could go, oh, I don't know, find her?"

"She could be anywhere in the city, and she's not answering my messages, so I don't know where to look to find her."

"You know…I am glad I got all the brains when we shared a womb. You really are a dense idiot."

"Fuck off!"

"You first, you're in *my* hotel room! Do you even remember why we're here right now?"

"What?"

"Humour me."

"We are on tour…? What the fuck is your point!"

"Who are everywhere we are and know our every move while we are on tour?" Charlie asks, patronising me.

"Staff?" I guess.

"Oh my god, you really are an idiot," Charlie grumbles in frustration. "Check with security! They will know where she is."

Fuck. I am an idiot.

"Asshole," I grumble, getting out of his bed.

"Yeah, yeah. Love you too," Charlie says half-heartedly, rolling back over and snuggling deeper into his blankets.

Leaving him to sleep, I walk down the hall and stop in front of the security guard by the elevator.

"Sir, can I help you?" he asks.

"Do you know where Ali is?"

"One moment," he replies before talking though his radio. "She is with Cecilia, Maverick, and the rest of Afterglow at a recording studio in town."

"Can you get me a lift there, please?"

"Of course, sir."

Seventeen - Alintia

WAKING up with Joel every morning has been heavenly, but we never get the chance to be alone. Today was meant to be a day off, but instead I am working in the studio with the band, Cecilia, and Maverick. He is only here to help Cecilia if she needs any assistance. With this being a new space, it can be hard for her to feel comfortable. Cecilia sent me a message moments after I woke up asking me to come and meet them so we can start recording a few new singles that we have only done live so far.

I thought she would want Joel to get the duet done, but he hasn't shown up yet, and we have been here for almost three hours now. Cecilia believes the process of recording music is an art form—and she is proving herself to be an asset to us. Being our manager and even producing some of the tracks with us, she is making the songs sound a hundred times better.

"Take a five-minute break," Cecilia says though our headsets.

Taking off my headset, I step out of the recording booth and make myself a coffee at the refreshments table.

"About time you got here!" Maverick says.

I glance around to see who he was talking to and meet the hazel eyes of Joel. Grinning, I walk over to him and give him a quick hug.

"I missed you," I say in a low voice to him.

"You didn't wake me." I can hear an edge of complaint in his tone.

"I tried," I chuckle, pulling back to look at him again. "You sleep like the dead. Besides, at least you got my note where I was."

"What note?"

"You didn't see it? Then how did you know where I was?"

"I asked the security guard. You seriously left me a note?"

"Yes," I giggle. "It was on the coffee table. On top of your lyric workbook. Figured you would be bound to look at that at some stage this morning."

"I was a little distracted this morning, waking up to an empty bed."

"Ah, so you admit it feels like shit?" I tease him.

"Yes, I relent. I was a dick. I get that now."

"At least you are here now," I sigh, falling back into his warm embrace. He drops a kiss to the crown of my head, and I feel myself melt into him.

"Can we talk?" Joel asks, and I instantly tense.

"Uh, sure." I turn back to the room, grateful to find no one has been watching us. "We are just gonna step out for a couple of minutes."

"Ok," Cecilia replies. "Joel, have her back in five minutes, ok? We only have the studio for the day, and I don't want you wasting all her time."

"Sure thing, warden," Joel says, giving her some brotherly teasing.

Stepping out of the room, Joel leads me into another recording booth, this one empty of anyone and their lurking ears and eyes.

"What's up?" I ask, keeping my distance from him and sitting down on the single couch in the room.

"We haven't really had the chance to talk about anything that has happened in the last week, I guess." He shrugs, and I relax only slightly.

"I suppose you're right. What did you want to talk about specifically?"

"Us."

"What's wrong with us?"

"Nothing, at least I hope not. I just mean like, are we dating? Are we exclusive? I just want to be on the same page."

"Do you not want to be exclusive?"

"What? No!" Joel shouts. "I mean, no to that, I want to be. I want you to be my girlfriend. I want you to meet my parents and come home to you every night. I want the world to know that we are together."

"I think you achieved that last one when you kissed me on stage in front of ten thousand fans and their cameras."

"Yeah, I guess," Joel laughs, walking over and sitting down on the couch next to me. "Are you ok with all that?"

"Yes, I would love to be your girlfriend Joel," I say softly.

"Then get over here!" Joel manhandles me until I am straddling his lap, hand gripping my waist as I curl my hands into his long hair and bring our lips together.

We kiss gently, our tongues caressing—nothing like the fiery kisses that have led us to sex, but still full of the same overpowering, overwhelming emotions. Joel sighs into my mouth, the tension in his body leaving him—giving me an odd sense of power and pride. I do that to him—for him—helping him relax and put him at ease.

"So, boyfriend?" I pull back only far enough to talk, but my lips graze his as I speak.

"Yes, girlfriend?" I feel his lips smile, turning up at the word.

"I was thinking," I say, leaning back now to meet his eyes. "Now that you are here, maybe we can work on the duet?"

"You think, aye?"

"Well yeah, it makes sense—the studio, the band is here. We never really discussed who was doing the music, but Maverick is here to help out for Fly By. And we can call the others down if you want, too?"

"I think that's a great idea."

"I know you already wrote your side, and the melody—so I have been playing around with my lyrics. I think they fit, but I want to run them by you."

"Will you sing them for me now?" he asks, hope on his face.

Singing a cappella is not something new to me, or singing for an audience of one, but something about this moment— sitting alone on top of my boyfriend, singing him a song about my love for him—has me feeling nervous.

"Don't laugh, ok?"

"I won't. I promise."

The look in his eyes gives me confidence to do this, and I don't want him to hear these words for the first time in front of everyone else. I close my eyes and begin singing to Joel.

I fell for your body, a damn work of art.

Your stuck in my mind, playing with my heart.

A tune on repeat, a bad metaphor I know.

I'm lusting after a vacant mind.

YOUR BODY IS **a sin that I wish to commit.**

I'm falling for an incubus from Hell's pit.

My mother warned me of men like you.

I want you under my flesh and I think you do too.

PARADISE, **ain't far from those devil eyes.**

And I'm terrified

That I'm still in love with you

Oh you

Paradise, I can't find it in strangers' thighs.

I keep coming back to you,

Oh you

You…

I finish the last note and hesitate to open my eyes, worried about what Joel's reaction is.

"Oh, Alintia." His voice is deep and full of emotion.

I peek at him from under my eyelashes, surprised to find his eyes watery.

"Joel?" I ask, looking at him fully now.

"Th-that was beautiful." He clears his throat. "No one has ever done anything like that for me before."

I grin sheepishly at him. "You liked it?"

"Oh, baby, I loved it—I love you."

I freeze on his lap. His hands flex against my hips where they have been grounding me since he deposited me here. Joel's eyes flare with panic.

"I-I didn't mean…" he stutters, trying to take it back.

"No, you can't take it back!" I protest, covering his mouth with my hand to stop him from saying anything further. "I know it's soon, and you don't want to scare me off, but I feel it too. I am falling in love with you, Joel Watson."

I feel his mouth turn into a huge smile, and I rip my hand away so I can see it. I tilt my head back, laughing at the ceiling, pure joy radiating through me. Joel places a soft and sweet kiss against my neck, quick like he couldn't resist doing it.

"Yo!" Chris calls through the door.

"Yeah?" I call back, laughter in my voice.

"Cecilia sent me to come get you, Ali. Time to get back to it."

I lean forward, giving Joel a lingering kiss as I step off his lap and begin straightening out my jeans and t-shirt.

"Come on then," I say, offering Joel my hand. He accepts it and I pull him up off the couch, and we continue holding hands as we go out into the studio.

"So, we were thinking—" Joel starts once we rejoin the others.

"That's dangerous," Maverick interjects, teasing his little brother.

Joel rolls his eyes and ignores him. "We were thinking we are ready to demo the duet, if you are ready for it?"

"You finished it?" Cecilia squeaks in excitement, her body almost humming.

"Yeah, we think we have. It might need a little of your input," I say to Cecilia, squeezing Joel's hand encouragingly. "But we think it's ready for an audience."

"Get in there, then!" Cecilia says, waving at the recording booth.

I grin at Joel and tug him into the room behind me. As we set up, I glance at Joel and cannot help but think this is something that I could get used to.

Eighteen - Alintia

IT'S the last night of our tour in Australia, and I have no idea where the time has gone. So much has changed within a matter of weeks, but I couldn't be happier.

It's also the night that Joel and I will perform our duet in front of a live audience on stage.

We finalised it in the recording studio last week, but the record label held off, thinking it would be better to debut it at the end of the Australian leg of the tour, giving everyone here time to stream it and love it before we return, and give the other countries time to get to know it before we get there on tour.

"Are you nervous?" Joel asks me. We are standing in his dressing room getting ready for the concert together.

"Not really. I am more so sad that this tour is over."

"Ah," Joel says, wrapping his arms around my waist, resting his head on my shoulder, and meeting my gaze in the mirror. "But it's not an ending, not really. We still have the other legs of the tour that we will get to spend together. And if you think that I will let you go after finally getting you—you are out of your mind."

I smile at him, leaning further into his embrace. "I am not letting you go either, Joel."

"I am also pretty certain that Reckless will want us to do more songs together. This song is going to go wild in the charts, only made better by our relationship. I know I would love to write more songs with you."

"I'm not sure if you can afford me," I joke, leaning back towards the mirror to finish applying my makeup.

Joel grips my hips, whipping me around to face him.

"I'll try my hardest," he promises in a breathless whisper against my mouth. Leaning forward, he presses his lips against mine, hard and fast, his tongue swooping in and tangling with mine. I will never get over this man. The sensation of his touch, both caressing and demanding at once. As my body goes lax in his embrace, the powder brush in my hand falls to the ground, startling both of us. We break apart at the noise, returning to reality.

"Well, we have a show to do," I say. Even though it's the last show, Joel is right—there are more things beginning than ending with this tour.

Joel picks up my dropped brush and places it back in my palm.

"I'll stop distracting you then, Miss Hawkins," Joel says, putting on an Elizabethan gentleman's voice and bowing to me.

"Thank you, Mr. Watson," I reply, equally faux primly, and curtsy in turn.

Joel leaves the bathroom, but I can hear him pottering around the dressing room getting himself ready too. I still haven't gotten over the fact that he—this marvellous, remarkable, and I'll admit sometimes asshole of a man—is *mine*. Even though he has fans all around the world who love him and vie for his attention, he is my boyfriend, my lover—just mine.

I apply the last of my makeup, fix up my hair, and I walk out to join Joel in the dressing room.

"You ready for this?" he asks me.

"Yes." I grin up at him, and he places a soft kiss on my lips, careful to not mess up my lipstick.

We head down the hallway, hand in hand, and a feeling of rightness washes over me. This is my life now. Performing in concerts for audiences of over ten thousand people, singing songs that I love. I never counted on finding a steady boyfriend—sure I had wanted it, but with my track record of dating I wasn't expecting anything this amazing.

The rest of Afterglow arrive at the stage the same time we do. We just signed our new contract with Reckless Tunez. We aren't on the same level as Fly By yet, but I think we really have chance of getting there. We've built ourselves up because of own work and talent, not just because I am Joel's girlfriend.

"Ok, let's do this!" I say, grinning at Jax, Chris, and Steph.

Joel brings my hand to his mouth, placing a kiss on the back of my hand before releasing me. "Give them a great show, baby."

"You know I will, love," I reply with a wink.

I pull out my phone, taking a photo of Joel and I together this time, and send it out to my family in my usual preshow message.

Me: Last show in Australia, can't believe how quickly this tour has gone. I have made new friends, a new connection, and new music. Missing you all, see you in a few days xx

"Ready?" a stagehand asks.

"Yeah!" I reply enthusiastically, stepping up to my microphone as the curtain pulls away, revealing us to the crowd's cheers.

"Ladies, gents, and all you lovely people here," I say into the microphone after the last song on our set, "we have a bit of a surprise for you tonight. We have loved performing for you, but we all know that you are here to see Fly By—and I don't blame you. That lead singer, whew!" I exaggerate fanning myself, flirting with the crowd a little. "He and I have been working together lately and have written a song that we would like to share with you tonight!"

The crowd breaks out in cheers, and the boys walk out on stage to join us. The stagehands wheel out a second set of drums for Charlie, Ethan heads over to the keyboard setup, and Maverick and Tom are holding their instruments. Joel walks directly to me, wrapping his arm around my waist and speaks into the microphone in his hand. "Thanks Ali, it has been great working with you, and I am sure that we will be doing much more together in the future!" he says with a wink. His tone heavy with insinuation.

"Honestly can't take rock stars anywhere," I jokingly admonish. Our flirty banter entertains the crowd as the others get set up.

"You love me here and you know it," Joel presses a kiss against my temple, and it takes everything in me to not close my eyes and sigh into the embrace.

"So," I say, addressing Joel and pretending that the crowd isn't there, "do you think they are ready to hear our new duet?"

Calls of "YES!" "YEAH!" and "PLEASE!" bounce around the concert hall.

"I'm not sure," Joel says, pretending like he couldn't hear them. "This song is pretty racy—I don't know if they are prepared for that."

The crowd keeps calling out, "YES! PLEASE!"

"I think they will be ok. Are you?" I ask, turning back to the crowd.

I get more "YES!" in response, and, indicating the band to start the music, jump into the duet with Joel. Joel begins, his husky voice washing over me, even if we are in front of thousands—he is singing only to me.

A devil in disguise, a demon manifest.

An excuse for me to fall in love.

You've used me and pulled me apart to

A shattered husk of a heart.

YOUR BODY IS **a sin that I wish to commit.**

I'm in love with a succubus deep in Hell's Pit.

I get down on my knees, oh baby please.

Take me, break me, vilify and ravage me!

PARADISE, **ain't far from those devil eyes.**

And I'm terrified

That I'm still in love with you

Oh you

Paradise, I can't find it in strangers' thighs.

I keep coming back to you,

Oh you

You…

I reach out and cup Joel's face, singing my section back to him.

I fell for your body, a damn work of art.

Your stuck in my mind, playing with my heart.

A tune on repeat, a bad metaphor I know.

I'm lusting after a vacant mind.

YOUR BODY IS **a sin that I wish to commit.**

I'm falling for an incubus from Hell's pit.

My mother warned me of men like you.

I want you under my flesh and I think you do too.

· · ·

PARADISE, **ain't far from those devil eyes.**

And I'm terrified

That I'm still in love with you

Oh you

Paradise, I can't find it in strangers' thighs.

I keep coming back to you,

Oh you

You...

Our voices meld together, joining for the bridge and the last chorus.

All I want is a taste that you can't give me.

A forbidden fruit that I need to bite into.

Open up to me and I'll give you my all.

A beautiful life with you not wanting for more.

FOR I'VE SCOURED **this world and I've found it lacking.**

For the thing that I need isn't worth having,

If it isn't with you then I can't have it.

And thus I'll falter and fade out of time,

YOU'RE **a sin that I've committed and I shall not repent.**

If you are the Devil then I'll tear down those gates,

I'll burn all the people that stand in our way,

and get on my knees for you.

PARADISE IS **within those devil eyes.**

And I'm terrified

That I'm going to lose you

Oh you

Paradise, I've given up in strangers' thighs.

I'll keep coming back to you,

Oh you

You…

We stand there, staring into each other's eyes as the song fades in a nostalgic 80's song style that Joel insisted the song should have—reminiscent of the 80's love ballads he grew up on—only inches between us, and the world around me falls away. All there is, is Joel. He is all I can see, all I can hear.

His lips quirk up in a smile. "Are you gonna kiss me or not?"

I lunge for him, my hands twisting into the soft cotton of his t-shirt and hauling him to me. His hands wrap around me to steady himself, his hands immediately dropping to palm my ass, as our lips crash together. Our tongues tangle in their own dance, our bodies pressed so tightly together I can feel his belt buckle digging into my stomach.

Joel is the first to pull back, and the moment our lips separate, sound rushes back in. The crowd is going wild.

"So, Mr. Watson," I whisper to him so our voices aren't picked up in the microphones, "would you sin for me?"

"Every day, for the rest of my life."

Grinning, I turn back to the crowd. "Thank you all for coming out and listening to us tonight. I will leave you in the capable hands of Fly By to rock your night away."

With a kiss to his cheek, I start to leave the stage.

"Ladies and gents, give it up for my girlfriend, my runaway girl, Ali and her band Afterglow!"

Grinning back at Joel, I mockingly curtsey to the crowd, blow him a kiss and step off the stage, joining Cecilia where she is sitting.

"So, what did you think?" I ask her, sitting down next to her and accepting a bottle of water from a stagehand.

"It was perfect. Exactly what I hoped for when I suggested to Reckless that we have you do a duet together," Cecilia says smugly.

"What? I thought the decision came from higher up?"

"Technically, they were the ones who gave the go ahead. But when you and I first met, I could sense there was a connection between you two and thought it would be explosive in a song. I knew there was something behind Joel's behaviour—I figured pushing you together might help resolve it. I didn't predict that you would fall in love with each other, but I am glad it worked out that way," she says, smiling widely at me.

"It's not quite love yet," I say, glad no one else is here to see my blush.

"Isn't it?" she teases.

"So that pushing about helping him get over 'that girl' was completely coincidence?" I ask, moving away from that word.

"A happy coincidence. At the time I didn't know you were the girl I thought he needed to get over."

Our conversation trails off as the boys start their set, sitting there in companionable silence as we watch our men do their thing.

Nineteen - Joel

"YOU DON'T NEED to be nervous," I assure Alintia, sliding my hand over hers and squeezing it gently.

We are in my car heading back to Orlo for Sunday lunch with the family. We only have a one-week break before we head off to America together, and we figured it was time we met each other's parents. We landed back in the Gold Coast this morning, finishing the Australian leg of the tour last night. The debut of "Sin for Me" was explosive. The studio version dropped live on all streaming platforms at midnight, and it is already trending.

"What if they don't like me?" she asks, keeping her eyes out the window. We are only a few streets away from my family home now.

"They will love you, if only for the fact that I love you and you make me happy. But they will absolutely accept you," I say.

I pull into their street, the cars for my brothers already here. We are probably the last to arrive because I took Alintia by her apartment first.

"You can do this," Alintia whispers to herself.

Smiling, I get out of the car, walking around and opening the door for her.

"I have never done this before," she admits to me.

"Gone to a rock star's house?" I joke.

"No. Met a boyfriend's parents. I have never been with them long enough to get to that stage."

If I have it my way, you will never have to meet a new boyfriend's parents again.

Holding on to her hand, I lead her up to the front door. I never knock here. Although I haven't lived here for a few years, this is my home, and I know that I am always welcome.

Opening the door, the contentedness of being home washes over me. I can smell my parents cooking. I can hear Tom and Ethan fighting over the PlayStation. Soon, I am sure, I will be able to hear someone playing music in the garage. Even though we are on break from tour—the music is a part of us. No matter where we go or what we do, it will always be there with us, even on our days off.

"Hey, we're here!" I call out, closing the front door behind us.

Mum rushes out of the kitchen, and it hits me just how much I have missed her over the last few weeks.

"Joel!" Mum flings her arms around my waist and burrows her head into my chest, not being able to reach too much higher.

Mum is a very eccentric woman, and that comes across in everything she does, and how she can dress. She is wearing her usual outfit of white linen pants, a bright tank top—

orange this time—and her hair is out and wild. She doesn't like when it looks all straight and controlled.

"Hey, Mum. I've missed you," I admit, wrapping my arms around her and dropping a kiss to the top of her hair. I linger in her hug for a moment longer before pulling back and reaching for Alintia's hand.

"Mum, this is my girlfriend, Alintia. Ali, this is my mum, Odette." She has loved Cecilia since the moment Maverick brought her home, and I can't help but hope she will feel the same way about my Alintia.

"It's a pleasure to meet you," Ali says softly.

"Oh, come here!" Mum says, wrapping her arms around Ali.

"She's a hugger," I stage whisper to Alintia.

"Joel! How's it going, mate?" Dad says, entering the room decked out in a hot pink apron that says, "I like my racks big, my butt rubbed, and my beef pulled" in black writing. Ethan bought that for him as a gag gift last Christmas, and I don't think he ever expected Dad to wear it. Dad thought it was hilarious though, and it resulted in him making jokes about Mum and barbequing that, as their sons, we found very inappropriate.

"I am good, Dad. How are you?" I ask, bringing him into a hug. He is about the same height as me and my brothers, whereas Mum is around five-foot-five.

"Good, mate, and who is this?" Dad asks, as if he isn't fully aware of who Ali is.

"This is Alintia, my girlfriend. Ali, this is Griffin," I say with a wide grin. He hates being called by his full name.

"Pfff, please. Call me Griff. Griffin makes me feel old," Dad grumbles, leaning in and kissing Ali on the cheek. "Are you guys ready to get your grill on?"

"Ugh, Dad!" Ethan groans from his position on the couch. "Go back to the lame dad jokes, those are better than these barbeque puns."

"Ah, but the 'lame dad jokes' don't get a reaction out of you guys," Dad replies with a smirk.

"Now Ali, come," Mum says, indicating she follow her into the kitchen. I can smell a potato bake cooking away in the oven, and the scents from the barbeque coming through the back door.

Mum draws Ali into a conversation, asking her all about her family and how she found her first tour while I pick up a knife to help Mum with the salad.

"I had a great time on tour. I was truly blessed to have that experience, and I am blessed to have found Joel, which I didn't expect at all."

"Aren't you just a sweetie," Mum says with affection in her eyes.

Dad comes back inside carrying a plate full of a smoked beef brisket, placing it in the centre of the dining table. Ali helps set the bread rolls and garden salad on the table while I bring in the coleslaw and roast corn, Mum following behind with the potato bake.

"BOYS!" Dad calls through the opening to the lounge room.

"Griff!" Mum scolds. She hates it when there is yelling all through the house.

As my brothers file into the room, I tug Alintia into my arms and drop a kiss to the top of her head. With my girl in my arms, surrounded by my family, I know I can do anything.

20

Epilogue - Charlie

COMING HOME IS a little bittersweet for me today. Gwen is just next door at her parent's house—but she doesn't want to see me. It has been verging on radio silence from her for the last three weeks, and I don't know how I can change it.

Other than my brothers, she is my best friend, and has been for almost fifteen years. Sure, I have been in love with her for almost seven of those—but she doesn't need to know that.

I am not sure how I can reach out to her again, especially since she has been adamant that she wants to have less contact with me, at least while her relationship is new.

My phone buzzes just as we are sitting down to Sunday family lunch, and I ignore it. It's surely not Gwen, and family time is family time. Besides, this is Ali's first time meeting Mum and Dad, and I want it to go well for her and Joel—I can see how much she means to him and he really deserves the best in life. My phone keeps incessantly buzzing, to the point of distracting me from the conversation.

"Excuse me, sorry, let me see what this is," I say to the table, pulling out my mobile.

The call goes to voice message the second I have it in my hand, but before I can even see who it was, my phone starts ringing again. It's the front desk at my and Joel's apartment building.

"Hello?" I answer the call.

"Oh, Mr. Watson. Thank god we got a hold of you," a flustered man says through the phone.

"Is everything ok? Is there something wrong with the apartment?" I ask, making eye contact with Joel across the table.

"N-n-no," he stutters. "I mean, there is nothing wrong with the apartment, but there is a delivery here for you."

"Oh, is that it? I will be back in the city in a few hours you can just leave it in my apartment like you guys normally do," I say, disgruntled that this was all the call was regarding. "Goodbye."

"W-w-wait!" he blurts.

"What?" I grunt in frustration.

"We can't just leave it in your apartment."

"Why?"

"Well, sir," he exhales in a rush, "it's a baby."

THE END

Interested in what happens next
with the Fly By Boys?

Stay tuned.
Charlie is up next with "Touch Me"!

Sin for Me

A devil in disguise, a demon manifest.
An excuse for me to fall in love.
You've used me and pulled me apart to
A shattered husk of a heart.

Your body is a sin that I wish to commit.
I'm in love with a succubus deep in Hell's Pit.
I get down on my knees, oh baby please.
Take me, break me, vilify and ravage me!

Paradise, ain't far from those devil eyes.
And I'm terrified
That I'm still in love with you
Oh you
Paradise, I can't find it in strangers' thighs.
I keep coming back to you,
Oh you
You…
I fell for your body, a damn work of art.

Your stuck in my mind, playing with my heart.
A tune on repeat, a bad metaphor I know.
I'm lusting after a vacant mind.

Your body is a sin that I wish to commit.
I'm falling for an incubus from Hell's pit.
My mother warned me of men like you.
I want you under my flesh and I think you do too.

Paradise, ain't far from those devil eyes.
And I'm terrified
That I'm still in love with you
Oh you
Paradise, I can't find it in strangers' thighs.
I keep coming back to you,
Oh you
You…
All I want is a taste that you can't give me.
A forbidden fruit that I need to bite into.
Open up to me and I'll give you my all.
A beautiful life with you not wanting for more.

For I've scoured this world and I've found it lacking.
For the thing that I need isn't worth having,
If it isn't with you then I can't have it.
And thus I'll falter and fade out of time,

You're a sin that I've committed and I shall not repent.
If you are the Devil then I'll tear down those gates,
I'll burn all the people that stand in our way,
and get on my knees for you.

Paradise is within those devil eyes.
And I'm terrified
That I'm going to lose you

Hear Me

Oh you
Paradise, I've given up in strangers' thighs.
I'll keep coming back to you,
Oh you
You…

Seen

I'm in a cold dark room surrounded by people I've never met.
Encompassed yet so alone. Hidden behind a mask my smile
shines through to appear that I'm alright.

All I want is someone's eyes to dissolve all I am, take me apart
piece by piece, put back all my fragments and...

See me! Help me! Step forward into the light tell me
everythings alright. Then one day, the world will! See me! And
accept all that Ive become before I come undone, so please
just.

I build walls so high I couldn't see the sky, tore apart my heart
so it wouldn't break. I can talk the talk and walk the walk but
I've never felt at home in my own skin.

All I want is someone to show me all I am, to show what I
could be, so I can...

See me! Help me! Step forward into the light tell me

everythings alright. Then one day, the world will! See me! And accept all that I've become before I come undone, so please let me.

Don't wait on me I'll never make it over. To self obsessed with how get over - all these years of hiding all that I am. I wanna break out and shout to the heavens!

I see me! I'll help me! Step forward into the light tell me everythings alright. Todays the one day, the world will! See me! And accept all that Ive become I'll never run away from me.....

Inverted

"Damn guys get a load this of this one, hey there sugar!"
I'm the type of guy that can bring you to you knees. Begging
"please please please!"
I'm not your lord or saviour but I'm hearing your prayers.
Tonight's all I care about is getting you out of that dress ...but
leave on those boots.

I'd love see the inside of you, would you like me too?

Did you wanna be, did you wanna be my baby?
Cause I wanna be, I wanna be your daddy!
I'm burning hot, gimme whatchu got and I'll lay it on real
smooth.
Ill take you down, I'll make you move, and I'll spin you round.
Inverted!

I've never seen a woman move the way that you do.
With your body so sweet that I'd never forget the taste too.
The things you do to my head, when your in my bed.

Inverted

Some would think that your sucking up for something......Oh
wait ...

Did you wanna be, did you wanna be my baby?
Cause I wanna be, I wanna be your daddy!
I'm burning hot, gimme whatchu got and I'll lay it on real
smooth.
Ill take you down, I'll make you move, and ill spin you round.
Inverted!

I thought I'd be the one using you, but it seems that we've
swapped
Making you my lil toy that I'd wind up and watch.
You've got a devilish tongue, that you've wrapped around me
and man "I hate it when she does that"
And now I'm so damn deep that I'll never leave.
So...

Cause your gonna be, your gonna be my baby.
And I wanna be, I wanna be your daddy!
I'm burning hot, gimme whatchu got and I'll lay it on real
smooth.
Ill take you down, I'll make you move, and I'll spin you round.
Inverted!
Oh ... We're Inverted!

Runaway

Brown heels, curly hair, eyes so blue you'd think they're the ocean.
I found you in a cafe downtown, my heartbeat stopped, and the world lost its sound.
Fell in love at first sight, don't know who you are but that's alright.
Are you even a fan of people like me? Long hair, dark clothes and all inked from my head to my feet...
Will you....

Runaway tonight! Let's runaway tonight
Runaway tonight! Let's runaway tonight

I know people might not like the way that you walk, the way that you dress,
but you're a best thing I've ever seen baby.
We'll be followed by paparazzi and cheap magazines, you don't gotta worry cause I'll show you the real me. So when they're following us we'll just...

Runaway

Runaway tonight! Let's runaway tonight.
Runaway tonight! Let's runaway tonight
And if they ever come knocking on our front door I'll go give
em what's for and make them ...
Runaway tonight! Go on runaway tonight.

We'll be Bonnie and Clyde, ride till we die. Make sweet love
every night.
Talk about life and the weight of it all. Drive with the top
down or fly to Nepal.
As long as we got each other, one way or another. There ain't
nothing in this life that's gonna bring us down. So let's just...

Runaway tonight! Let's runaway tonight
Runaway tonight! Let's runaway tonight
And I'll be ok, even though I watched you runaway from me,
I'll be here waiting for you so we can...
Runaway tonight! Let's runaway tonight
Runaway tonight! Let's runaway tonight

Acknowledgments

Where to even begin? Another book written, and plenty more on the way!

Firstly, thank you to all of my readers. I really wouldn't be here without you. You, along with my characters, give me the motivation to keep on writing an publishing.

Thank you again to my brother, Lukasz Muller who wrote the Fly By songs along with me, all of their songs are included in the post script of this book.

To my lovely betas, Bec and Isabou. Thank you for being my sounding board, listening to all my crazy thoughts and encouraging me to get it out onto paper!

Thank you to my friend, Tia, who completed the sensitivity read for this story. I pride myself on writing well rounded characters, representing all types of people. One of my goals with writing Alintia was ensuing that I did not fall into any stereotypes or prejudices—while also ensuring that the main part of the story wasn't focused on the fact that Ali is Aboriginal. I wanted to write her in a way that her race doesn't solely define her or the story, and show that there is more to her, while also showing that there are HEA's for everyone.

And last, but certainly not least, to my fiancé—Hayden. You are the love of my life, every one of my MMCs has an element of you in them. You are my biggest supporter, never doubting and always there for me to cheer me on when I can celebrate my sales and reviews. You are a silent warrior, sometimes you barely say anything—but you are fierce, determined, caring and all-round amazing. I will love you, and our little family, forever.

About the Author

Heidi grew up and lives in south-west Sydney, Australia, with her marvellous fiancé, Hayden. Heidi is a dog mum to a beautiful, attention loving Labrador, Daisy. Heidi is 25 and has 2 brothers and a sister.

Heidi had difficulties learning and maintaining the standard literacy and numeracy requirements in school, until she found her love for reading. It all started with a cringe worthy obsession over a certain Edward Cullen, which has fuelled Heidi to go on to reading 200+ books a year.

With a passion for reading, Heidi began writing short stories, and has always had an overactive imagination. Heidi comes across as a loud, boisterous person, who is actually a shy girl terrified of rejection. This fear held Heidi captive for a long time and prevented Heidi from sharing any of her work - until 2020.

With three previous books published, and a series in progress, Heidi cannot wait to share the inner desires of her mind with you all.